THE PROFESSOR WAS A THIEF

L. RON HUBBARD

THE
PROFESSOR
WAS
A THIEF

Published by
Galaxy Press, LLC
7051 Hollywood Boulevard, Suite 200
Hollywood, CA 90028

Printed in the United States of America.

ISBN-10 1-59212-351-1
ISBN-13 978-1-59212-351-3

Library of Congress Control Number: 2007927522

CONTENTS

STORIES FROM PULP FICTION'S GOLDEN AGE

A ND it *was* a golden age.

The 1930s and 1940s were a vibrant, seminal time for a gigantic audience of eager readers, probably the largest per capita audience of readers in American history. The magazine racks were chock-full of publications with ragged trims, garish cover art, cheap brown pulp paper, low cover prices—and the most excitement you could hold in your hands.

"Pulp" magazines, named for their rough-cut, pulpwood paper, were a vehicle for more amazing tales than Scheherazade could have told in a million and one nights. Set apart from higher-class "slick" magazines, printed on fancy glossy paper with quality artwork and superior production values, the pulps were for the "rest of us," adventure story after adventure story for people who liked to *read*. Pulp fiction authors were no-holds-barred entertainers—real storytellers. They were more interested in a thrilling plot twist, a horrific villain or a white-knuckle adventure than they were in lavish prose or convoluted metaphors.

The sheer volume of tales released during this wondrous golden age remains unmatched in any other period of literary history—hundreds of thousands of published stories in over nine hundred different magazines. Some titles lasted only an issue or two; many magazines succumbed to paper shortages during World War II, while others endured for decades yet. Pulp fiction remains as a treasure trove of stories you can read, stories you can love, stories you can remember. The stories were driven by plot and character, with grand heroes, terrible villains, beautiful damsels (often in distress), diabolical plots, amazing places, breathless romances. The readers wanted to be taken beyond the mundane, to live adventures far removed from their ordinary lives—and the pulps rarely failed to deliver.

In that regard, pulp fiction stands in the tradition of all memorable literature. For as history has shown, good stories are much more than fancy prose. William Shakespeare, Charles Dickens, Jules Verne, Alexandre Dumas—many of the greatest literary figures wrote their fiction for the readers, not simply literary colleagues and academic admirers. And writers for pulp magazines were no exception. These publications reached an audience that dwarfed the circulations of today's short story magazines. Issues of the pulps were scooped up and read by over thirty million avid readers each month.

Because pulp fiction writers were often paid no more than a cent a word, they had to become prolific or starve. They also had to write aggressively. As Richard Kyle, publisher and editor of *Argosy*, the first and most long-lived of the pulps, so pointedly explained: "The pulp magazine writers, the best of them, worked for markets that did not write for critics or attempt to satisfy timid advertisers. Not having to answer to anyone other than their readers, they wrote about human beings on the edges of the unknown, in those new lands the future would explore. They wrote for what we would become, not for what we had already been."

Some of the more lasting names that graced the pulps include H. P. Lovecraft, Edgar Rice Burroughs, Robert E. Howard, Max Brand, Louis L'Amour, Elmore Leonard, Dashiell Hammett, Raymond Chandler, Erle Stanley Gardner, John D. MacDonald, Ray Bradbury, Isaac Asimov, Robert Heinlein—and, of course, L. Ron Hubbard.

In a word, he was among the most prolific and popular writers of the era. He was also the most enduring—hence this series—and certainly among the most legendary. It all began only months after he first tried his hand at fiction, with L. Ron Hubbard tales appearing in *Thrilling Adventures, Argosy, Five-Novels Monthly, Detective Fiction Weekly, Top-Notch, Texas Ranger, War Birds, Western Stories,* even *Romantic Range.* He could write on any subject, in any genre, from jungle explorers to deep-sea divers, from G-men and gangsters, cowboys and flying aces to mountain climbers, hard-boiled detectives and spies. But he really began to shine when he turned his talent to science fiction and fantasy of which he authored nearly fifty novels or novelettes to forever change the shape of those genres.

Following in the tradition of such famed authors as Herman Melville, Mark Twain, Jack London and Ernest Hemingway, Ron Hubbard actually lived adventures that his own characters would have admired—as an ethnologist among primitive tribes, as prospector and engineer in hostile climes, as a captain of vessels on four oceans. He even wrote a series of articles for *Argosy,* called "Hell Job," in which he lived and told of the most dangerous professions a man could put his hand to.

Finally, and just for good measure, he was also an accomplished photographer, artist, filmmaker, musician and educator. But he was first and foremost a *writer,* and that's the L. Ron Hubbard we come to know through the pages of this volume.

This library of Stories from the Golden Age presents the best of L. Ron Hubbard's fiction from the heyday of storytelling, the Golden Age of the pulp magazines. In these eighty volumes, readers are treated to a full banquet of 153 stories, a kaleidoscope of tales representing every imaginable genre: science fiction, fantasy, western, mystery, thriller, horror, even romance—action of all kinds and in all places.

Because the pulps themselves were printed on such inexpensive paper with high acid content, issues were not meant to endure. As the years go by, the original issues of every pulp from *Argosy* through *Zeppelin Stories* continue crumbling into brittle, brown dust. This library preserves the L. Ron Hubbard tales from that era, presented with a distinctive look that brings back the nostalgic flavor of those times.

L. Ron Hubbard's Stories from the Golden Age has something for every taste, every reader. These tales will return you to a time when fiction was good clean entertainment and the most fun a kid could have on a rainy afternoon or the best thing an adult could enjoy after a long day at work.

Pick up a volume, and remember what reading is supposed to be all about. Remember curling up with a *great story*.

—Kevin J. Anderson

KEVIN J. ANDERSON *is the author of more than ninety critically acclaimed works of speculative fiction, including The Saga of Seven Suns, the continuation of the Dune Chronicles with Brian Herbert, and his* New York Times *bestselling novelization of L. Ron Hubbard's* Ai! Pedrito!

THE PROFESSOR
WAS A THIEF

PREFACE

I T was about two o'clock in the afternoon and Sergeant Kelly, having imbibed a bit too much corned beef and cabbage at lunch, was dozing comfortably at his desk. He did not immediately hear the stumbling feet of Patrolman O'Rourke, but when he did, he was, in consequence, annoyed.

Sergeant Kelly opened his eyes, grunted, and sat slowly forward, hitching at his pants which he had unbuckled to ease his ballooning stomach.

His eye was offended at first by Patrolman O'Rourke's upset uniform and then, suddenly, interested. And what sergeantly eye would not have been? For Patrolman O'Rourke's mouth was slack and his eyes could have been used as bowling balls. He ran into a spittoon and heeded its thundering protest and departure not at all. Bracing his tottering self against the desk without changing his dazed expression, O'Rourke gulped:

"It's gone."

"Well!" said Sergeant Kelly. "Don't stand there like a jackanapes! Speak up! *What's* gone?"

"The Empire State Building," said Patrolman O'Rourke.

CHAPTER ONE

NO one knew why he was called Pop unless it was that he had sired the newspaper business. For the first few hundred years, it appeared, he had been a senior reporter, going calmly about his business of reporting wholesale disaster, but during the past month something truly devastating had occurred. Muttering noises sounded in the ranks.

Long overdue for the job of city editor, lately vacated via the undertaker, Pop had been demoted instead of promoted. Ordinarily Pop was not a bitter man. He had seen too many cataclysms fade into the staleness of yesterday's paper. He had obit-ed too large a legion of generals, saints and coal heavers to expect anything from life but its eventual absence. But there were limits.

When Leonard Caulborn, whose diapers Pop had changed, had been elevated to city editor over Pop's decaying head, Pop chose to attempt the dissolution of Gaul in the manufactures of Kentucky. But even the latter has a habit of wearing away and leaving the former friend a mortal enemy. Thus it was, when the copy boy came for him, that Pop swore at the distilleries as he arose and looked about on the floor where he supposed his head must have rolled.

"Mr. Caulborn said he hada seeyuh rightaway," said the copy boy.

Pop limped toward the office, filled with resentment.

Leonard Caulborn was a wise young man. Even though he had no real knowledge of the newspaper business, people *still* insisted he was wise. Hadn't he married the publisher's daughter? And if the paper didn't make as much as it should, didn't the publisher have plenty of stockholders who could take the losses and never feel them—much, anyway.

Young and self-made and officious if not efficient, Caulborn greeted Pop not at all, but let him stand before the desk a few minutes.

Pop finally picked up a basket and dropped it a couple inches, making Caulborn look up.

"You sent for me?" said Pop.

"I sent for you— Oh, yes, I remember now. Pending your retirement you've been put on the copy desk."

"My *what*?" cried Pop.

"Your retirement. We are retiring all employees over fifty. We need new people and new ideas here."

"Retirement?" Pop was still gaping. "When? How?"

"Effective day after tomorrow, Pop, you are no longer with this paper. Our present Social Security policy—"

"Will pay me off about twenty bucks complete," said Pop. "But to hell with that. I brought this paper into the world and it's going to take me out. You can't do this to me!"

"I have orders—"

"You are issuing the orders these days," said Pop. "What are you going to do for copy when you lose all your men that know the ropes?"

6

"We'll get along," said Caulborn. "That will be all."

"No, it won't either," said Pop. "I'm staying as reporter."

"All right. You're staying as reporter then. It's only two days."

"And you're going to give me assignments," said Pop.

Caulborn smiled wearily, evidently thinking it best to cajole the old coot. "All right, here's an article I clipped a couple months ago. Get a story on it."

When Caulborn had fished up the magazine out of his rubble-covered desk he tossed it to Pop like a citizen paying a panhandler.

Pop wanted to throw it back, for he saw at a glance that it was merely a stick, a rehash of some speech made a long while ago to some physics society. But he had gained ground so far. He wouldn't lose it. He backed out.

Muttering to himself he crossed to his own desk, wading through the rush and clamor of the city room. It was plain to him that he had to make the most of what he had. It was unlikely that he'd get another chance.

"I'll show 'em," he growled. "Call me a has-been. Well! Think I can't make a story out of nothing, does he? Why, I'll get such a story that he'll *have* to keep me on. And promote me. And raise my pay. Throw me into the gutter, will they?"

He sat down in his chair and scanned the article. It began quite lucidly with the statement that Hannibal Pertwee had made this address before the assembled physicists of the country. Pop, growing cold the while, tried to wade through said address. When he came out at the end with a spinning head he saw that Hannibal Pertwee's theories were not supported by anybody but Hannibal Pertwee. All other information, even to Pop, was so much polysyllabic nonsense. Something about transportation of freight. He gathered that much. Some new way to help civilization. But just how, the article did not tell—Pop, at least.

Suddenly Pop felt very old and very tired. At fifty-three he had ten thousand bylines behind him. He had built the *World-Journal* to its present importance. He loved the paper and now it was going to hell in the hands of an incompetent, and they were letting him off at a station halfway between nowhere and anywhere. And the only way he had of stopping them was an impossible article by some crackbrain on the transportation of freight.

He sighed and, between two shaking hands, nursed an aching head.

CHAPTER TWO

A pavement-pounding reporter is apt to find the turf trying—and so it was with Pop. Plodding through the dismal dusk of Jersey, he began to wish that he had never heard the name of Hannibal Pertwee. Only the urgency of his desire to keep going had brought him thus far along the lonely roads. Grimly, if weakly, he at last arrived at a gate to which a Jerseyite had directed him.

With a moan of relief he leaned against a wire-mesh fence and breathed himself to normalcy. It wasn't that he was getting old. Of course not! It was just that he should have worn more comfortable shoes.

He looked more observantly about him and became interested. Through this factory fence he could see a house, not much bigger than an architect's model, built with exactness which would have been painful to a more aesthetic eye than Pop's.

The fence itself next caught his interest. He fingered the steel mesh with wonder. At the top the poles bent out to support three strands of savage-looking barbed wire. Pop stepped back and was instantly smitten by a sign which shouted:

1,000,000 VOLTS
BEWARE!

Pop felt a breeze chill him as he stared at his fingers. But they were still there and he was encouraged. Moving toward the gate he found other signs:

BEWARE OF THE LIONS!

Pop searched anxiously for them and, so doing, found a third:

AREA MINED!

And:

TRESPASSERS BURIED
FREE OF CHARGE!

Uncertain now, Pop again stared at the tiny house. It began to remind him of a picture he had seen of Arizona's gas chamber.

But, setting his jaw to measure up to the threats around him, he sought the bell, avoiding the sign which said:

GAS TRAPS

And the one which roared:

DEATH RAYS
KEEP OUT!

He almost leaped out of his body when a voice before him growled: "What is your business?"

Pop stared. He backed up. He turned. Suspiciously he eyed the emptiness.

At last, rapidly, he said, "I want to see Hannibal Pertwee. I am a reporter from the *New York World-Journal*."

There was a click and a square of light glowed in a panel. For seconds nothing further happened and then, very slowly, the gate swung inward.

Boldly—outwardly, at least—Pop marched through. Behind him the gate clicked. He whirled. A little tongue of lightning went licking its chops around the latch.

It took Pop some time to permanently swallow his dinner. He glared around him but the strange change in the atmosphere soon registered upon his greedy senses.

Here the walk was only a foot wide, bordered by dwarf plants. What Pop had thought to be shrubbery was actually a forest of perfect trees, all less than a yard tall but with the proportions of giants. Here, too, were benches like doll furniture and a miniature fountain which tinkled in high key. Sundials, summerhouses, bridges and flowers—all were tiny, perfect specimens. Even the fish in the small ponds were nearly microscopic.

Pop approached the house warily as though it might bite. When he stood upon the porch, stooping a little to miss the roof, the door opened.

Standing there was a man not five feet tall, whose face was a study of mildness and apology. His eyes were an indefinite blue and what remained of his hair was an indefinite gray. He was dressed in a swallowtail coat and striped pants and wing collar, with a tiny diamond horseshoe in his tie. Nervously he peered at Pop.

"You are Mr. Brewhauer from the *Scientific Investigator*?"

"No. I'm from the *New York World-Journal*."

"Ah."

"I came," said Pop, "to get a story on this lecture you handed out a couple months ago."

"Ah."

"If you could just give me a few facts, I should be very glad to give you a decent break."

"Oh, yes! Certainly. You must see my garden!"

"I've just seen it," said Pop.

"Isn't it beautiful? Not a bit like any other garden you ever surveyed."

"Not a bit."

"Such wholesome originality and such gigantic trees."

"Huh?"

"Why, over a thousand feet tall, some of them. Of course, trees don't ordinarily grow to a thousand feet. The tallest tree in the world is much less than that. Of course, the Aldrich Deep is 30,930, but then no trees grow in the ocean. There, now! Isn't the garden remarkable? I'm so sorry to walk you all over the place this way, but I have recently given my cars to charity."

"Hey," said Pop. "Wait. We haven't been anywhere."

"No, indeed not. My garden is only a small portion of what I have yet to show you. Please come in."

Pop followed him into the house, almost knocking off his hat on the ceiling. The house was furnished in somewhat garish fashion and, here again, everything was less than half its normal size, even to the oil paintings on the walls and the grand piano.

"Please be seated," said Hannibal Pertwee.

Somehow Pop squeezed himself into a chair. There was a tingling sensation as though he was receiving a rather constant shock. But he paid it no heed. Determined to get a story, he casually got out his cigarette case and offered Hannibal a smoke.

The little man started to refuse and then noticed the case. "What an unusual design!"

"Yeah," said Pop, and pressed the music button. "The Sidewalks of New York" tinkled through the room.

"Fascinating," said Hannibal. "What delicate mechanism! You know, I've made several rather small things myself. Here is a copy of the Bible which I printed." And in Pop's hand he laid the merest speck of a book.

Pop peered at it and somehow managed to open it. Yes, each page appeared to be perfectly printed. There was a slight tingling which made him scratch his palm after he had handed the volume back.

"And here is a car," said Hannibal, "which I spent much time constructing. The engine is quite perfect." And thereupon he took the inch-long object and poked into it with a toothpick. There was a resultant purr.

"It runs," said Pop, startled.

"Of course. It should get about a hundred thousand miles to the gallon. Therefore, if a car would make the trip and if it could carry enough gas, then it could go to the moon. The moon is only 238,857 miles from Earth, you know." And he smiled confidently. He had forgotten about the car and it started up and ran off his hand. Pop made a valiant stab for it and missed. Hannibal picked it up and put it away.

13

"And here is a car," said Hannibal, "which I spent much time constructing. The engine is quite perfect." And thereupon he took the inch-long object and poked into it with a toothpick.

"Now I must show you around," said Hannibal. "Usually I start with the garden—"

"We've seen that," said Pop.

"Seen what?"

"The garden."

"Why," said Hannibal, "I said nothing about a garden, did I? I wish to show you my trains."

"Trains?"

"Have you ever played with trains?"

"Well—I can't say as I have. You see, Mr. Pertwee, I came about that lecture. If you could tell me what it is about—"

"Lecture?"

"That you made before the physics society. Something about moving freight."

"Oh! 'The Pertwee Elucidation of the Simplification of Transportational Facilities as Applying to the Freight Problems of the United States.' You mean that?"

"Yes. That's it!"

"I'm sorry, but Mr. Pertwee does not refer to the subject now."

"Mr.— Wait, aren't *you* Mr. Pertwee?"

"Yes, indeed. Now about my trains—"

"Just some comment or other," pleaded Pop. "I couldn't understand just what it was all about."

"There's nothing half so lovely as a train," said Mr. Pertwee, almost firmly.

Pop took out his case and lighted a cigarette.

"Would you mind pressing that button again?" said Pertwee.

15

Once more the worn mechanism tinkled out its music. When it had done, Hannibal took the case and inspected it anew with great attention.

"You said something about trains," said Pop.

"Pardon?"

Pop took back his case and put it firmly away. "You spoke of trains. There may be a story there."

"Oh, there is, there is," said Hannibal. "But I don't talk about it, you know. Not with strangers. Of course you are not a stranger, are you?"

"Oh, no, indeed," said Pop, mystified because he could see no bottle about. "But let's get on to the trains."

Hannibal bounced eagerly up and led his caller through the house, pausing now and then to show other instances of things done very small.

Finally they reached the train room and here Pop stopped short in amazement. For here, spread out at their feet, were seemingly miles of track leading off in a bewildering tangle of routes.

"My trains," said Hannibal, caressingly.

Pop just kept staring. There were toy stations and semaphores and miniature rivers and roads and underpasses and sidings and switches. And on the tracks stood a whole fleet of freight cars in a yard. Engines stood about, ready to do the switching. The roundhouses were crammed with rolling stock and, in short, nearly every type of equipment used was represented here.

Hannibal was already down on his knees at a switchboard.

He grabbed up a top hat and plonked it on his head and then beamed at Pop.

"Cargo of strawberries for Chicago," said Hannibal. He threw half a dozen switches. The engines in the freight yard came to life and began to charge and puff and bang into cars, making up a train without any touch from the operator except on the control board.

"That bare space away over there is Chicago," said Hannibal.

Pop saw then that this room was vast enough to contain a replica of the United States and realized with a start that these tracks were, each one, a counterpart of an actual railroad line. Here were all the railway routes in the United States spreading over a third of an acre!

"This is New York," said Hannibal, indicating another bare space. "Only, of course, there isn't anything there yet. Now here we go!"

The freight, made up, began to move along the track faster and faster. It whistled for the crossings and rumbled over the rivers and stepped into a siding for a fast freight to go by, took on water and finally roared into the yard beside the bare space which was Chicago. Here it was broken up and other engines began to reform it.

In the space of two hours, Pop watched freight being shunted all over the United States. He was excited about it, for he had never had a chance to play with trains as a boy and now it seemed quite logical that they should interest him as a man.

Finally Hannibal brought the cars back to the New York

yard and broke up the last train. With a sigh he took off his hat and stood up, smiling apologetically.

"You must go now," said Hannibal.

"Look," said Pop. "Just give me some kind of an idea of what you were talking about in that article so I can mention it in the paper."

"Well—"

"I'll do you some good," said Pop.

"Do you understand anything about infinite acceleration?"

"Well, no."

"Or the fourth dimension?"

"Welllllllllll . . ."

"Or Einstein's mathematics?"

"No."

"Then," said Hannibal, "I don't think I can explain. *They* would not believe me." And he laughed softly. "So, you see, you wouldn't either. Good night."

And Pop presently found himself outside the gate, confronted once more with the long walk to the station and the long ride back to New York.

A fine job he'd done. No story.

Still— Say! Those trains would make a swell yarn. A batty little scientist playing with toy railroads— Sure. He'd do it. Play it on the human-interest side. Great minds at leisure. Scientist amuses self with most complete model road in the world— Yes, that was it. Might do something with that.

But he'd never get far with it.

Trudging along he reached for his cigarette case. He fumbled in other pockets. Alarm began to grow on him. He couldn't find it! More slowly he repeated the search.

Hurriedly then he tore back to the gate and shouted at the house. But the only reply he got was printed on the sign:

TRESPASSERS BURIED
FREE OF CHARGE!

CHAPTER THREE

POP, it might be said, was just a little proud of having turned out a presentable story where no story had been before. And, feeling the need of a little praise, he finished off his story the following morning and took it to Caulborn personally.

Caulborn, in a lather of activity which amounted to keeping half the staff enraged, pushed up his eyeshade—which he wore for show—and stared at Pop with calculated coldness.

"Well?"

"That story you sent me out on," said Pop, putting the sheets on Caulborn's desk. "You didn't think there was any story there. And you were right as far as news was concerned. But human interest—"

"Humph," said Caulborn, barely glancing at the type. He was, in truth, a little annoyed that Pop had gotten anything at all. When Caulborn had taken this job he had known very well that there were others in the office who had more seniority, more experience, and therefore a better claim.

"You call this a story?" said Caulborn. "You think we print anything you care to write? Go back to the copy desk." And so saying he dropped the sheets into the wastebasket with an emphatic gesture of dismissal.

Pop was a little dazed. He backed out and stood on the sill for seconds before he closed the door. A hurrying reporter jostled him and was about to rush on when he saw Pop's expression.

"Hey, you look like you need a drink."

"I do," said Pop.

The reporter glanced at Caulborn's door. "So he's making it tough for you, is he? The dirty rat. Never mind, Pop, when better newspapermen are built they'll all look like you. Something will break sooner or later—"

"I'm leaving tomorrow."

"Say, look now! Don't quit under fire. You know what ails that guy? He's scared, that's all. Scared of most of us and you in particular. Why, hell's bells, you belong in that chair. We're losing money, hundreds a day, and when it gets to thousands the publisher himself will get wise—"

"I'm being laid off," said Pop.

"You? For God's sake!"

Pop wandered back to his desk. Two other reporters came over to commiserate with him and curse Caulborn, but Pop didn't have anything to say. He just kept on pulling old odds and ends out of his desk, throwing many of them away but making a packet out of the rest.

"You're not leaving today, are you?" said a third, coming up.

"What else can I do?" said Pop.

And he went on cleaning out his desk, looking very worn and old and quiet. He scarcely looked up when Caulborn passed him, on his way out to lunch.

It was about one o'clock and he was just tying a string around his belongings—a pitifully small package to show for all his years in this city room. The phone rang on the next desk and Pop, out of habit, reached across for it.

"Gimme rewrite," barked an excited voice.

"I'll take it," said Pop suddenly.

"This's Jenson. I'm up on the Drive. Ready?"

Pop raked some copy paper to him and picked up a pencil. He was a little excited by the legman's tone. "Ready."

"At twelve-forty-five today, Grant's Tomb disappeared."

"Huh?"

"Get it down. The traffic on the Drive was at its noon-hour peak and the benches around the structure were filled with people. When, without warning, a rumble sounded, the alarmed populace—"

"To hell with the words," cried Pop. "Give me the story. How did it happen?"

"I don't know. Nobody knows. There are half a dozen police cars around here staring at the place Grant's Tomb was. I was about a block away when I heard shrieks and I came tearing down to find that traffic was jammed up and that people were running away from the place while other people ran toward it. I asked a nursemaid about it and she'd seen it happen. She said there was a rumbling sound and then suddenly the tomb began to shrink in size and in less than ten seconds it had vanished."

"Was anybody seen monkeying with it?" said Pop, feeling foolish instantly.

"A chauffeur said he saw a little guy in a swallowtail coat tear across the spot where the tomb had been."

"How many dead?"

"Nobody knows if anybody is dead."

"Well, find out!"

"How can I find out when everybody that was sitting on the steps and all completely disappeared?"

"What?"

"They're gone."

"Somebody is crazy," said Pop. "No bodies?"

"No tomb."

"I got this much," said Pop. "You hoof it back there and get stories from the witnesses." He hung up and whirled to shout down the line of desks, "Grant's Tomb's gone! Get Columbia on the phone. We got to have a statement from somebody that knows his stuff. You, Sweeney, grab an encyclopedia and see if anything like this ever happened before. Morton, grab a camera and get out there for some pictures. Dunstan! You go with Morton and find the relatives of the people that have vanished along with the tomb. Get going!"

Nobody asked any questions beyond a stammer of incredulity. Nobody thought of tearing out to find Caulborn. Sweeney, Morton, Dunstan and others went into a flurry of activity.

"Branner!" cried Pop into the interoffice phone. "Start setting up an extra. We'll be on the street in half an hour. Second extra in an hour and a half with pictures."

"Is this Pop?"

"Yeah, this is Pop. What are you waiting for?"

"Okay. Half an hour it is."

"Louie, get some shots of Grant's Tomb out of the files and rush them down to Composing." Pop pulled his old typewriter toward his stomach and his fingers began to flash over the keys. Hunt and punch it was, but never had a story rolled so swiftly. In five minutes it was streaming down to Composing.

Pop got up and paced around his desk. He rumpled his graying hair and looked unseeingly out across the city room. He had pinch-hit as night editor so often that he did not question his authority to go ahead. And still nobody thought of Caulborn.

Shortly a damp proof was rushed up. The copy boy hesitated for a moment and then laid it on Pop's desk. Pop looked it over. "Okay. Let it run."

The boy loped away and Pop, reaching for a cigarette, again missed his case. Instead he hauled up a limp package and lighted a match. The phone rang somewhere.

"Take it, Pop," said a reporter.

Pop took it.

"Who's this?" said Pop.

"Freeman. Grab your pencil."

"Got it," said Pop, beginning to tingle at the tone of the legman.

"The Empire State Building disappeared about five minutes ago."

"Right," said Pop.

"I'm down at precinct— About three seconds ago a cop came staggering in with the news. I haven't had a chance to look."

"Get right down there and see," said Pop. "Grant's Tomb vanished just before you called."

"Check."

Pop put down the phone and dashed over to the window. But in vain he searched the skyline for any sign of the Empire State Building. "Gone," he said. The human being in him was appalled. The newspaperman went into action.

"Goodart," roared Pop, "get a camera down to the Empire State. It's disappeared."

"Check," said Goodart, dashing away.

"Copy boy!" yelled Pop. And into the phone, even while he started the second story, he yelped, "Branner. Limit the first extra. Get set for a second. Story coming down. The Empire State Building has disappeared."

"Okay," said Branner.

"Get some pictures down to Branner on the Empire State," shouted Pop. His fingers were blurring, so fast they raced over the keys.

"New York is going piece by piece," said a reporter. "Oh boy, what a story!"

"Call the mayor, somebody!" said Pop. "Tell him about it and ask him what he means to do."

"Check," said a cub eagerly.

"No such incident in the encyclopedia," reported Sweeney.

"Unprecedented," said Pop. "Lawson and Frankie! You

two get cameras and rush downtown to be on hand in case any other big buildings exit. Copy boy!"

And the second story was on its way to Composing. And still nobody remembered Caulborn.

Pop went back to the window, but the Empire State was just as invisible as ever.

"Columbia says mass hypnotism or hysteria," said a girl.

"Get their statement," said Pop.

"Got it."

"Dress it up and shoot it down."

"Check."

Pop walked around his desk. Again he reached for his cigarette case and was again annoyed to find it gone. He lighted up, frowning over new angles, one eye hopefully on the phone.

"Find out how many people are usually in the Empire State," said Pop.

"Check," said a reporter, grabbing a phone.

"Don't try to call the Empire State!" said Pop. "It isn't there!"

The reporter looked silly and changed his call to the home of a director of the Empire State.

Certain that the story would keep breaking, Pop was not at all surprised when Frankie called.

"Pop! This's Frankie. Pennsylvania Station's gone!"

"Penn— Full of people?"

"And trains and everything!" cried Frankie. "There's nothing there but a hole in the ground. I was lucky, about a block away and saw it happen! You said *big* so I figured Pennsylvania—"

27

"The story!"

"Well, there was a kind of rumble and then, all of a sudden, the station seemed to cave into itself and it was gone!"

"Statements!"

"A little guy in a swallowtail coat almost knocked me down running away. He was scared to death. Everybody was trying to get away. And right on the corner one of our boys was shouting our first extra. The whole building just disappeared, that's all. People, trains, everything. You ought to see the hole in the ground—"

"Get statements and rush your pictures back here. Don't be a damned photographer all your life."

"Okay, Pop."

"Pennsylvania Station," yelped Pop. "Tim, get this for rewrite. About five minutes ago, Pennsylvania Station disappeared—people, trains, everything. There's nothing but a hole in the ground. There was a rumble and then the thing vanished. Seemed to cave into itself but there is no debris. It's gone. All gone."

"Okay, Pop," said Tim, his mill beginning to clatter.

"Copy boy!" shouted Pop, pointing at Tim. "Pictures of Pennsylvania Station!" He grabbed a phone. "Branner! Keep adding to that extra. We got pictures coming of Pennsylvania Station. It's gone."

"Penn— Oh boy, what a story!"

Pop hung up. "Angles, angles—" The phone rang.

"This is Lawson. I just heard that Grand Central disappeared. I'll get down there for some pictures and call you back."

"Pennsylvania Station just went," said Pop.

"The hell," said Lawson.

"On your way," said Pop.

"Gone," said Lawson.

Pop reached for another phone which was clamoring.

"This is Jenson again. I been checking all the angles. About a thousand people saw it disappear when—"

"What? What's gone now?"

"Why, Grant's Tomb—"

"Hell, kill it. The Empire State, Pennsylvania and Grand Central have gone since then. Get down here with your photographer."

"I haven't seen him. Did you send one?"

"Get down here. Do you think this is a vacation? Bring in your yarns. They'll just make our fourth extra."

"Okay, Pop."

"Got a statement from the mayor. He's yelling sabotage," said the cub. "He says he's phoning the governor to call out the militia. He says they can't do this to his town."

"Banner for extra number three," barked Pop into the phone. "Mayor Objects. Calls Out Militia. Story coming down." He jabbed a finger at the cub's typewriter. "Roll it out and spread it thick. They'll be half-panicked by now. Stab in a human-interest angle. Make 'em take it calm."

"Check," said the cub nervously.

Pop walked around his desk and again reached for his cigarette case, to again discover that it was missing. "Angles—two men with swallowtail coats—"

Pop whirled, "Eddy! Take this lead. Mystery man seen

in two catastrophes. A small man with a swallowtail coat was present today at both the vanishing of the tomb and Pennsylvania Station. Was seen to run across place where tomb had been and collided with one of our reporters just after Pennsylvania disappeared. Got it?"

"Check."

Pop went over to the window. The Empire State was still gone. A thought was taking definite form in his mind now. For some reason he kept harking back to Hannibal Pertwee. Railway stations, cigarette case, swallowtail coat—

Freeman came dashing up. "She's sure gone."

"What?"

"The Empire State. There's nothing but a hole in the ground. There were umpteen thousand people inside and there's no sign of them—"

"Okay! Do me a story about the state of the city—how calm they're taking it. Smooth them down. Third extra on its way and you'll make the lead in the fourth."

"Right," said Freeman. "But you oughta seen that cop—"

"Don't tell me. I don't buy the paper. Write it."

"Okay, Pop."

Pop turned back to his desk. He was so preoccupied that he did not see a dark cloud come thundering through the city room.

Caulborn, with a copy of the first extra in his hands, bore down upon what was obviously the center of the maelstrom.

"Did you do this?" he cried, shaking the extra under Pop's nose.

"Sure. What about it?"

30

"Why didn't you call me? You know where I eat lunch! How do you know this story is true? What do you mean spreading terror all over the town? How is it that we get a paper out so quick when there's nobody else on the streets? If this is a farce, then we'll be in Dutch plenty. Civil and criminal actions—"

"It takes guts to run a paper," said Pop coldly.

"If that's what it takes, you've got too many. Now we've got to check everything we've printed. If you've got another extra on the rollers, we'll have to kill it and find out if—"

"The third extra is on the street," said Pop.

Caulborn stared, growing angry. "And you took the authority without even *trying* to find me?"

"A story has got to go when it's hot," said Pop.

"All right! *All right!* And you ran this one so hot that you're driving New York into a panic! Get out!"

"What?"

"I said get out!" towered Caulborn. "You're through, finished, washed up. Today instead of tomorrow!" And, nursing his injured importance, Caulborn flung off to his office.

The city room was very quiet.

Pop stood for a little while and then, with a shrug, picked up the package on his desk.

"Well," he sighed, "it was fun while it lasted."

"You're going to take him at his word?" said somebody. "Just because you were smart enough not to wait? He's just sore because you did it so swell—"

"Maybe," said Pop.

"You're going to quit like this?" said Freeman.

"No. Not like this," said Pop.

"Whatcha going to do?" said the cub.

Pop hefted his package. He looked grim.

CHAPTER FOUR

AT dusk Pop approached the fortress of Hannibal Pertwee. But this time he did not lean against the fence or spend time in reading signs. True, he could not miss:

BEWARE OF THE LIONS!

but, having seen none on his previous visit, he refused to be alarmed. In fact, he was so unswerving of purpose that nothing short of lightning itself could have stopped him and he had an antidote for that.

At a garage he had managed to separate himself from five dollars he could ill afford, an electrician from a pair of insulated gloves, and the heaviest pair of wire cutters he could carry.

Breaking and entering would be a very serious offense, but he was first going to give Hannibal a chance.

For several minutes he waited dutifully at the gate, hoping that the mysterious voice would again speak. But this time it did not and the house remained as dark as it was small.

"You asked for it," muttered Pop.

Very painstakingly he inspected the latch. Then he donned the rubber gloves and took the cutters and went to work. In a few minutes the gate was swinging open, leaving its latch behind.

Oh, if this hunch he had was wrong!

He marched through the miniature forest down the miniature path and ducked to mount the porch. But there his purpose was eased.

Hannibal opened the door and gazed sadly at him.

"It will be so *much* work to repair that gate," said Hannibal.

"Well . . . uh . . . you see—"

"I was very busy. You are Mr. Frothingale from the *Atlantic Science Survey*, are you not?"

"I'm from the *World-Journal*," said Pop.

"You're sure you are not from the railroad company?"

"Ah," said Pop.

"Well—I am very sorry but I can't ask you in tonight. I am so busy."

"I . . . er . . . came after my cigarette case," said Pop.

"Cigarette case?"

"Yes. I lost it when I was here before. I would dislike having to part with it permanently."

"Oh, that is very shocking. Did you lose it here?"

"I had it when I was here and didn't have it after I left."

"Mightn't you have dropped it in the garden?"

"I had it while I was in the house. You don't mind if I come in and look, do you?"

"Why . . . er—"

But Pop was already shouldering past Hannibal Pertwee and the little man could not but give way. However, Hannibal skipped to the fore and guided Pop into the minute living room.

"I was sitting here in this chair," said Pop, looking under it.

Hannibal fidgeted. "Isn't it lovely weather?"

"Swell," said Pop. "You don't mind if I look elsewhere?"

"Oh, yes! I mean no! I am very busy. Really, you will have to go."

"But my cigarette case," said Pop, edging toward the train room, "is very valuable to me."

"Of course, of course. I appreciate your predicament. But if I had seen it and if I find it— Oh, dear, what am I saying?"

"Well," said Pop, suddenly crafty, "I won't trouble you further. I can see how upset you are." And he extended his hand. "Goodbye, Mr. Pertwee."

Eagerly Hannibal grasped the offered hand. Swiftly Pop yanked Hannibal close to him and gave him an expert frisk. The cigarette case leaped out of Hannibal's pocket. Pop looked at it with satisfaction.

"I wonder," said Hannibal, distrait, "how that got there?"

"So do I," said Pop. "And now if I could inspect your trains again—"

"Well . . . yes. All right. Just come this way." And he stepped through the door.

Pop was so close behind him that he almost got cut in half when the door slammed shut. There was the rumble of a shot bolt and Pop's weight against the door had no effect at all. He swore and dashed for the hall. Another door slammed there. Pop stood glaring through the walls at Hannibal. Then he got another idea and rushed outside to take a tour of the house. But there was nothing to be seen.

For two hours Pop prowled in the garden. But the night

35

was cold and Pop was hungry and, at last, he had to be content with his victory in recovering his case. He went off up the road in the direction of the station.

Grumbling to himself, he stood on the platform, waiting for a train to carry him back to New York. He could swear that there was some connection between the forest, the miniature car, the trains and the vanished buildings.

"Dja hear about them things disappearin' in N'York?" said a loafer.

"Yeah," said Pop.

"Awful, ain't it?" said the loafer.

"Yeah," said Pop.

"It's them Nazis," said the loafer.

Pop took out his cigarette case. It still contained several cigarettes so, evidently, Hannibal did not smoke. Pop lit up. He was about to replace the case when he wondered if any harm had come to it. He pressed the music button. No sound came forth.

"Damn him," said Pop. "Broke it." Well, he could have it fixed. Hannibal, the loon, had probably worn it out.

The train came at last and Pop settled himself for a doze. He could think best when he dozed. But his neighbor wasn't sleepy.

"Ain't that awful what them Reds did in New York? I hear that people are runnin' around trying to lynch all the Reds they know about. 'Course some don't believe it was the Reds, and I hear tell the churches is full of people prayin'. I'm goin' in to see for myself, but I'm tellin' you, you won't catch *me* walkin' into no buildings."

"Yeah," said Pop.

The train lippety-clicked endlessly, saying the same thing over and over: "Pop's through, Pop's through, Pop's through."

About eight he wandered out of the station to straggle haphazardly uptown. He was trying to tell himself that he was glad he was through. No more chasing fire engines for him. What a hell of a life it was. Never any regular sleep, always on the go, living from story to story. Well! Now he could settle down and rest awhile. Yes, that was the ticket. Just rest. There was that farm his sister had left him. He'd go up there in the morning. Place probably all falling to pieces but it would be quiet. Yes, a helluva life for a man. He'd followed the news for years and now all the stories he had covered were lumped into one chunk of forgetfulness—and he was as stale as yesterday's newspaper. What had it ever gotten him? Just headaches.

Shuffling along, head down, hands deep in his jacket pockets, he coursed his way to Eighth Avenue. From far off came a thin scream of a police siren. Pop stopped, instantly alert. The clang of engines followed, swooping down a side street near him. He raced up to the corner and watched the trucks and police cars stream by full blast. He whirled to a taxi and then paused, uncertain. Gradually he lost his excitement until he was again slumped listlessly. Far off the police sirens and bells dwindled and faded into the surflike mutter of the city.

"Taxi, buddy?"

Pop glanced toward the hack driver. He slowly shook his head and pulled out his cigarette case. He lighted up and puffed disconsolately. A saloon was nearby and he wandered into it to place a foot on the rail.

"Rye. Straight," said Pop.

The British-looking barkeep pushed out a glass and filled it with an expert twist of his wrist. Pop downed the drink and stood there for a while staring morosely at his reflection in the mirror behind the pyramided wares.

"Fill it up," said Pop.

The barkeep did as bidden. "Ain't that awful about them buildings and all?" he said the while. "The wickedness of this city is what brought it on. Just yesterday I says to a gent in here, I says, 'A town as sinful as this—'"

Pop took out his cigarette case. "Yeah."

"'A town as sinful as this cannot meet but one fate in the mighty wrath—'"

SWOOsssh!

Pop was jarred out of his wits.

The whole bar had vanished!

The whole bar, complete with tender!

The mirrors were still there, but that was all!

A drunk who had been sitting at a side table looked unblinkingly in the direction of the phenomenon and then, with great exactness, lifted his glass and spilled the contents on the floor. Unsteadily he navigated to the street.

Pop's news-keen mind examined all the possibilities in sight. Was it possible that someone had come in that door and done this? Had Hannibal followed him?

Absently he started to pay for his drink, coming to himself only when he saw for certain that he no longer leaned on the bar. He looked at the floor where the planks were patterned as the bar had stood. And then Pop received another shock.

There was the bar!

About an inch long!

Almost lost in a crack between the flooring!

Hastily he picked it up, afraid of hurting it. He could barely make out the bartender who did not seem to be moving. Pop put the thing in a small cardboard box he found in the refuse and then stowed it carefully in his pocket.

This opened up a wide range of thought and he needed air in which to think. He went out into the street.

Why was he so certain that it was Hannibal? He understood nothing of that man's plans and certainly there were thousands of swallowtail coats in New York City. But still—

This bar had dwindled in size. Was it not possible, then, that the buildings had done likewise? And if they had, mightn't they still be there? He mulled this for a long time, standing at the curb, occasionally hearing the wonder of a would-be customer in the saloon.

"Taxi?" persisted the driver.

"Yeah," said Pop. But before he got in, his abstraction led him to take out his cigarette case and light up. Then he entered the cab. "I want to go to the place Grand Central Station was."

"Okay, buddy," said the cabby.

He pondered profoundly as he waited for lights, and when the driver let him out near the police cordon which had been placed around the hole, he thought he had a glimmering of the meaning behind this series of events.

He paid and strolled along the line.

"Awful, ain't it?" said another spectator.

"Yeah," said Pop. He edged up to an officer. "I'm from the *World-Journal*. I want to examine that hole from the bottom."

"Sorry. Can't be done. I got strict orders."

A few minutes later, Pop was wandering about the hole. The street lights were sufficient for his inspection and, very minutely, he covered every inch of the ground. Then, finding nothing, he again risked bunions by doing it all over, again without result. He got out and walked away toward the site of the Empire State.

On the way he paused and bought some cigarettes, filling his case. When he had finished he wandered on down the avenue.

But his inspection of the hole where the Empire State had stood left him once more without clue. He was very weary and muddy when he had finished, for it was difficult walking.

He stood once more at the curb, determined to make his inspection complete.

"Taxi?"

Pop took out his case and started to extract a cigarette.

"Tax—"

SWOOsssssh!

And the cab folded into itself with such rapidity that Pop's eye could not follow.

Pop trembled.

He shut his eyes and counted to ten.

When he opened them the cab was still gone.

Then he looked more closely at the pavement and stooped

down. Here was the cab, a little less than an inch long and proportionate in the other two dimensions.

Pop put it in his cardboard box.

But nobody was near him. Evidently no one had seen this happen to the cab. And if Hannibal had sneaked up and caused it, there had been neither sign nor sound of his approach.

Maybe—maybe Hannibal wasn't guilty.

Maybe New York would keep right on disappearing!

To keep his sanity Pop vowed to complete his inspection. He moved to the next cab in the line in which the driver was dozing. The cabby woke with a start and reached automatically back for the door.

"I want to go to Pennsylvania Station," said Pop. And then, finding he still held the cigarette case in his hand, again opened it to take out another cigarette.

SWOOsssssh!

And this second cab was gone!

Pop began to tremble violently. His heart was beating somewhere near his tonsils. With a quick glance around he reached down and picked up the cab and slid it into his box.

"Hey, you," said a loitering cop. "What you doin'?"

"Pi . . . pickin' snipes," said Pop hurriedly.

"Well, get along."

Pop got without further waiting. It was quite clear to him now who was doing this. Himself! The cigarette case! Hadn't it jerked a little whenever these things had gone?

And wasn't he guilty of murder if these drivers and the bartender were dead?

41

When he was on a dark street he surreptitiously inspected the case by the faint glow of a shop window.

But there wasn't anything unusual about it. Pop looked around and found a trash can. If this case was doing it, it certainly could make this trash can dwindle. Pop pushed the opening button. Nothing happened. He pushed the music button. Again nothing happened.

He breathed a sigh of relief. Then he was wrong about this. It wasn't his cigarette case, after all. Somebody was following him, that was it. Somebody was sneaking up and doing these things to him. Well! He'd walk around and keep close watch and maybe it would happen once more. When his attention was distracted by the case, this other person— Sure, that was the answer.

Pop, feeling better, walked on to the next avenue. He took his stand on the corner near a large apartment house. This was fair game. And when the other person came near, he would take out his case and then, *bow!* grab the malefactor and drag him back to the paper for interview.

In a few minutes a fellow in very somber clothes came near. Pop took out his cigarette case and started to open it.

SWOOsssssh!

And the apartment building was gone!

Pop was shaken up by the vibration of its going but he did not lose his presence of mind. He snatched the bystander and bore him to earth.

The full light of the street lamp shone down.

He had captured a minister of the gospel!

Very swiftly Pop got away from there, leaving the minister

staring after him and then, seeing the hole where a building had been, praying.

By a circuitous route, Pop came back to the hole. He almost broke a leg getting down into it, so steep were the sides. But he forgot that when he found the tiny thing which had been a building. It looked like a perfect model, about five inches high. Pop, hearing a crowd gather on the street, got out of there, stuffing the building in his pocket. There was a sting to the object which was very uncomfortable.

All Pop's fine ideas had gone glimmering now. It *was* the case. It had to be. And to test it out he had probably slain hundreds, maybe thousands, of people. But his news sense was soon uppermost again.

At a safe distance from the site he again inspected the case. He pressed first one button and then the other and still nothing happened. It shook his orderly process of thought. He went on his way, case in hand, and found himself in a commercial street where great drays were parked. He went on. Before him was the waterfront.

A packing case stood upon a wharf. Pop chose it for a test and stood there for some time, pushing the case's buttons. But the packing case stayed very stubbornly where it was.

And then, quite by accident, Pop pushed both buttons at once!

SWOOsssh!

The liner which had been at the pier abruptly vanished!

There was a snap as the after lines went. There was a small tidal wave as the seas came together.

Pop had missed his aim!

43

He almost broke a leg getting down into it, so steep were the sides.
But he forgot that when he found the tiny thing which had been
a building. It looked like a perfect model, about five inches high.

He had gotten over being stunned by now. His first thought was to snatch the hawser which had not parted. He hauled it swiftly in. The ship was barely attached to the line. Very carefully Pop looked at the tiny boat, perfect in all details, but less than three inches long. He looked hurriedly about and shoved it into his pocket.

A steward was running in circles on the dock, yelling, "They've stole it! They've stole it! Help, murder, police! They've stole it!"

That "murder" set badly with Pop. He got out of there.

Ten minutes later he was in a phone booth. The night editor's voice boomed over the wire.

"Joe, this is Pop. Look, I've got a bar, two taxis, an apartment building and an ocean liner in my pocket. Stand by for an extra about midnight."

"You—huh? Sleep it off, Pop. And drink one for me."

"No, no, no!" cried Pop.

But the wire was dead.

Pop walked out of the booth, turned around and walked into it again. He dropped his nickel and began a series of calls to locate his man.

World-Journal," said Pop at last. "I want Barstow of Pennsylvania Railroad."

"This is Barstow. But I've given out statements until I'm hoarse. Call me tomorrow."

"You'll be at the *World-Journal* in two hours if you want your station back."

"Call me tomorrow," repeated the voice. "And lay off the stuff. It ain't good for you." There was a click.

Pop sighed very deeply.

So they wouldn't believe him, huh? Well, he'd show 'em! He'd show 'em!

And he loped for the station.

CHAPTER FIVE

I won't," said Hannibal, definite for the first time in his life. They sat in Caulborn's office and the clock said ten. Caulborn had not yet come in.

Hannibal Pertwee showed signs of having been mauled a bit. And even now he tried to make a break for the door. Pop tripped him and set him back on the chair.

"It's no use," said Hannibal. "I won't tell you or anybody else. After what they did to me, why should I do anything for them?"

In the center of the room sat a gunnysack. Carefully wrapped up within it were some items Pop had found occupying the vacant spaces in the vicinity of "New York" on Hannibal Pertwee's toy railway system.

"I'll have you for burglary," said Hannibal. "You can't prove anything at all. What if I do have some models of buildings? Can't I make models of what I please? And they're just models. You'll see!"

"What about those people you can see in them?" said Pop.

"They're not moving. Can't I make people in model form, too?"

Pop was alternating warm and chill, for he knew he was dabbling in very serious matters. Anxiously he looked at the clock. As though by that signal, Caulborn came in.

47

Caulborn had had a drink too many the evening before and he was in no condition to see Pop.

"What? You here again?"

"That's right," said Pop. "And I have—"

"There's no use begging for that job. We don't need anybody. Get out or I'll have you thrown out." And he reached across the desk for his phone.

Pop's handy feet sent Caulborn sprawling. Pop instead pushed the button.

"Send in Mr. Graw," said Pop, calling for the publisher.

"I'll blacklist you!" cried Caulborn. "You'll never work on another paper!"

"I'll take my chances," said Pop.

Mr. Graw, very portly, stepped in. He saw Pop and scowled. Caulborn was dusting off his pants in protest.

"What's this?" said Mr. Graw.

"He won't get out," said Caulborn. "He sent for you. I didn't."

"Well, of all the cheek!"

Pop squared off. "Now listen, you two. I been in this business a long time. And I know what a story is worth. You're losing money and you need circulation. Well, the way to get circulation is to get stories. Now!"

"I won't," said Hannibal.

On the table Pop laid out the four objects from the gunnysack: the Pennsylvania Station, Grand Central, Grant's Tomb and the Empire State. Then from his jacket he took the bar, the two taxis, the apartment house and the steamship.

"I won't!" cried Hannibal, attempting another break. Once more Pop pushed him back to the chair.

"What are these?" said Mr. Graw.

"Just what you see. The missing buildings," said Pop.

"Preposterous! If you have gone to all this trouble just to make some foolish story—"

Pop cut Mr. Graw's speech in half. "I've gone to plenty of trouble, but not to have anything made. These are the real thing."

"Rot," said Caulborn.

"I won't!" said Hannibal.

"Well, in that case," said Pop, "I'll make you a proposition. If I restore these to their proper places, can I have my job back—permanently?"

"Humph," said Mr. Graw. "If you can put back what this city has lost, I'll give you your job back. Yes. But why waste our time—"

"Then call Mr. Barstow of the Pennsylvania Railroad," said Pop. "You get him over here on the double and I'll put the buildings back."

"But how—"

Again Pop cut Mr. Graw down. "Just call, that's all. You can't afford to run the risk of losing this chance."

"If you're talking nonsense—" growled Mr. Graw. But he put through the call.

Caulborn was licking his lips in anticipation of what he would have done to Pop. What Caulborn had suffered in loss of pride yesterday could all be made up today. He'd show Graw!

It was an uncomfortable wait, while Hannibal protested at intervals and Caulborn rubbed his hands. But at last Mr. Barstow, in a sweat, came loping in.

"You called me, Graw? By God, I hope you've got news."

Graw pointed at Pop. "This idiot claims to have your station. He says this is it."

Barstow snatched up the "model" of Pennsylvania. It stung his hands and he put it back. He turned to Pop. "Is this a joke? That's a perfect replica, certainly, but—"

"Look," said Pop, "this is Hannibal Pertwee, probably the smartest scientist since Moses."

"Oh, you," said Barstow.

"So you know him," said Pop.

"He used to bother us quite a bit," said Barstow. "What is it now?"

"Ah, we get somewhere," said Pop. "Barstow, if this gentleman replaces your Pennsylvania Station and these other objects, will you make a contract with him?"

"About his ideas on freight?" said Barstow. "I don't know which is the craziest statement, that you'll restore the buildings, or that anything he can think up will affect our freight. But go ahead."

Pop yanked out a slip of paper. "I typed this. Sign it."

Smiling indulgently, Barstow signed the agreement. Graw and Caulborn shrugged and witnessed it with their names.

"All right," said Pop to Hannibal. "This is what you used to be begging for. You've got it now. Go ahead."

And indeed Hannibal Pertwee had undergone a change. All trace of sullenness was gone from his face, replaced by growing hope. "You mean," he said to Barstow, "that you'll really consider my propositions? That you may utilize my findings?"

50

"I've said so in this paper," said Barstow impatiently.

Hannibal rubbed his hands. "Well, you see, gentlemen, my idea was to reduce freight in size so that it could be shipped easily. And so I analyzed the possibilities of infinite acceleration—"

"Spare the lecture," said Pop. "Get busy. They won't understand anything but action."

"Ah, yes. Action. May I have the cigarette case?"

Pop handed it over.

"You see, you turn it upside down and—"

"Wait!" cried Pop. "My God, you almost made them come back in here. You want to kill all of us?" Hastily he hauled Hannibal outside, taking the bar and a taxicab with him.

"Now," said Pop, setting them down in a cleared space.

Hannibal caressed the case. "It was very ingenious, I thought. I had been waiting for this very thing. Apparatus would have been noticed, you see, but this was perfect. One can stand on the edge of a crowd and press the buttons, both together, and the atomic bubble within is set into nearly infinite acceleration. It spins out and engulfs the first whole object it embraces and sets it spinning in four dimensions. Of course, as the object spins at a certain speed, it is accordingly reduced in size. Einstein—"

"Just push the buttons," said Pop.

"Oh, of course. You see, to stop the object from spinning we have merely to engulf it with an atomic bubble spinning in four dimensions, all opposite to the first—"

"The buttons," said Pop.

Hannibal turned the case around so that it would open down. He pointed it in the general direction of the tiny taxi.

"It compresses time as well as space," continued Hannibal. "I just release the bubble—"

swoooOOSH!

The taxi increased in size like a swiftly inflated balloon. The *tick-tick-tick* of its engine was loud in the room. The cabby finished opening the door and then turned to where he had last seen Pop.

"What address, buddy?" and then he saw his surroundings. He stared, gulped, looked at the ring of reporters and office men and hastily shut off his engine, shaking his head as though punch-drunk.

"Now the bar," said Pop.

Hannibal pushed the buttons again and, suddenly—

swoooOOSH!

The bar was there, full size.

The British bartender finished filling the glass with an expert twist of his wrist. "And I says, 'A sinful city like this will sooner or later—'" He had been turning to put away the bottle. But now he found no mirrors, only the reaches of the city room. His British calm almost deserted him.

Pop handed the drink to the cabby who instantly tossed it down.

"Now we better not have a bar in this place," said Pop, "if I know reporters. Cabby, you and the barkeep step back here out of the way. Do your stuff, Hannibal."

SWOOssssh!

Stories
from the
Golden Age
by L. Ron Hubbard

Join the Stories from the Golden Age Book Club Today!

Yes! Sign me up for the Book Club (*check one of the following*) and each month I will receive:

○ One paperback book at $9.95 a month.
○ Or, one unabridged audiobook CD at the cost of $9.95 a month.

Book Club members get FREE SHIPPING **and handling** (applies to US residents only).

Name   (please print)

If under 18, signature of guardian

Address

City   State   ZIP   Telephone

E-mail

You may sign up by doing any of the following:
1. To pay by credit card go online at www.goldenagestories.com
2. Call toll-free 1-877-842-5299 or fax this card in to 1-323-466-7817
3. Send in this card with a check for the first month
   payable to Galaxy Press

To get a FREE Stories from
the Golden Age catalog check here ○
and mail or fax in this card.

Thank you!

Subscribe today!
And get a FREE gift.

For details, go to www.goldenagestories.com.

For an up-to-date listing of available titles visit www.goldenagestories.com

Stories from the **Golden Age** by L. Ron Hubbard

BUSINESS REPLY MAIL
FIRST-CLASS MAIL   PERMIT NO. 75738   LOS ANGELES CA

POSTAGE WILL BE PAID BY ADDRESSEE

GOLDEN AGE BOOK CLUB
GALAXY PRESS
7051 HOLLYWOOD BLVD
LOS ANGELES CA 90028-9771

Click, click.

SWOOsssssh!

And both bar and taxi were toy-sized instantly. The cabby began to wail a protest, but Pop shoved the tiny car into his hands.

"We'll make it grow up shortly," said Pop. "Down in the street. Frankie! You and Lawson get some cameras. Freeman, you call the mayor and tell him to gather round for the fun. Sweeney, you write up an extra lead, telling the city all is well. I'll knock out the story on this—"

"Oh, no, you won't," said Graw.

"Huh?" said Pop. "But you said, in front of witnesses—"

"I don't care what I said. I've suddenly got an idea. Who got out those extras so fast yesterday?"

"Pop did!" yelled Sweeney, instantly joined by a chorus.

Graw turned to Caulborn. "At first I believed you. But when I got to thinking it over after I found out how fast they really had come—"

"He didn't mean nothin' by it," said Pop. "He's just a little young."

"Pop," said Graw, "you can't have his job."

"Well, I didn't say—"

"Pop," said Graw, "I've got a better spot for you than that. You're managing editor. Maybe you can make this son-in-law of mine amount to something if you train him right."

"Mana . . . managing editor?" gaped Pop.

"I'm going to slip out of the job," said Graw. "I need rest. And so, Mr. Managing Editor, I leave you to your editions."

The roof-raising cheer which went up from half a hundred throats about them made Pop turn lobster-color. Savagely he faced around.

"Well?" said Pop. "What are you waiting for? We got an extra edition to get out and that means work. Hannibal, you trot along with Frankie and Lawson. They'll help you put them buildings back. And listen, Frankie, don't miss any shots." Hastily he scribbled out the addresses where ship and taxi belonged and then shooed them on their way.

Pop took up the package he had left at the switchboard. He went into the office marked "Managing Editor" and laid his belongings on the desk. He shed his coat, rolled up his sleeves and reached for the phone.

"Copy boy!" he shouted.

"Okay, Pop."

BATTLE OF WIZARDS

BATTLE OF WIZARDS

T HE humans were outnumbered and the council was grave. No one had asked them here to this dark valley on the galaxy's rim. No one had pleaded for their arts. They had come and nothing short of miracles would let them stay.

The Mineralogy Service wanted Deltoid. Their chief had reported to the Galactic Council that Deltoid contained an almost unlimited supply of catalyst crystals in a natural state, a fact which would reduce the cost of freighter fuel manufacture by two-thirds. No one had argued with the need. The Galactic Council had sent for the Navy and had told the Navy to "safeguard" a mining expedition to Deltoid. The Navy had refused. A shot fired in the presence of catalyst crystals would wipe out the planet and therefore the project.

An order, then, had wandered through dusty corridors to a small, forsaken office in the Military Defense Building of the capital to lie amongst fly-specked papers on a scratched desk. A bored chief of section had given it to Angus McBane and Angus had offered a few faint suggestions about overdue leave. But the leave was two standard years late anyway and Angus took the smudged sheet to supply. The office of Civil Affairs did not rate very high and what he got was third- and fourth-hand.

They loaded the *Argus 48* with five months' supplies, put aboard thirty marines and eighteen sailors who had been found a disgrace to the service and gave the ship routine clearance.

Rusted and dented amid the fine shining vessels of the important classifications, the *Argus 48* lay for twelve standard hours after release patching up a starboard port which had connected with a meteor and then fifteen more trying to get circulation into the jet cooling system. There was some raillery from the mechanics of the government base: the *Argus 48* was sailing under a CA and couldn't expect anything more.

Twenty-three days later they landed on Deltoid in a valley indicated by the original survey, "high-walled and impossible of land assault, sparse in game but containing the bulk of the beings that inhabit this system." The valley was about a hundred and fifty leagues in diameter. They made their preliminary salutations and then Angus McBane came to council with the high chiefs of the realm.

Angus was a Civil Affairs officer. Nominally he was a colonial officer, but three years of special training and five more of service in CA had somehow removed him from the ordinary. He forgot to polish his buttons now. He had become gentle with years of dealing with less sentient races. He had spent a long time out beyond the last scout field and the life had changed him from the ordinary.

He clung to a stick as a symbol of a gentleman. But his topee was a disgrace and his tunic pockets bulged and he had found that mastodon-hide boots were best.

He squatted down at the council, cross-legged, his

black-and-gold stick across his knees, his bold Scot face sharply white in contrast to his uncut hair, his wise eyes bright in the firelight. Behind him knelt Dirk, who had the largest mechanical sense and the least conscience of any non-com in the service.

The place smelled bad and the people smelled worse. They were humanoid and one would have thought them more than that until he looked at their feet and hands. Where there were claws, there should have been nails. And there was a deal too much hair on them. But they were sentient, oddly so, and their speech, even through the translating filter, was full of startling strength.

"You say you come to bring us blessings," said the ruling chief. "We have blessings. You say you can teach us many things. We know many things. You say you have much to give and you give nothing!"

The chief threw the trinkets into the fire, a magnifying glass and a chain of gold coins. Angus McBane showed no emotion about it. He looked at the men there, saw signs of disease and malnutrition, looked back at the chief.

"I can show you many ways to grow good food. I can cure a thousand sicknesses. I can prepare aids which will make your work less. I bring peace and plenty. Do not despise my gifts."

"You want this valley," said the chief, rearing up seven feet tall and glaring. "You want my people should enter your slavery. Your looking-over vessels came. This was not the first time we had seen your race. Five men of the looking-over vessel did not go back. We have no reason not to detain six."

59

"You must not talk like children," said Angus, aware that knives had shifted. "We want the rights to mine a rock on your planet. You may retain your own government. But I have many things to give. I can show you how to raise food, good food, lots of food, food that is good to eat. I can build you ways to bring water into your villages. I can take away your sicknesses. I can do many powerful things for you and you will not have to pay."

The tribal chief expanded his chest and glared round him at his fellow councilmen. He read their mood.

"What power do you have that we do not have?" said the chief.

"It is a thing we call science," said Angus patiently. "With it we build such things as the ship in which we came. It will do many great things. It can make light appear in the night and it can keep beds dry when it rains. It can produce better children and it can make everyone wise. It can—"

"You say this *science* is powerful. Perhaps," said the chief, glowering, "you do not know that we also have a thing which is power."

"What is this thing?" said Angus.

A queer clacking sound came and a sleek, fat fellow rose from beside the fire. He grinned with superiority and then, with a glance at the chief, waved his hand through the air.

Instantly a banner of light glowed there and then began to materialize into a form. Several near the fire scuttled back. Sergeant Dirk's rum-bleared eyes shot wide. A woman was taking form there, comely save for her claws. She floated upon the air and then abruptly dropped to the floor. She sat up, dazed, looked at the fire-painted faces, at Angus, and hurriedly rushed from the council hut.

The sleek, fat youth sat down.

"Power," said the chief. "We have power. Is science greater than this magic?"

Angus McBane pushed at a live coal with his cane. He looked up after a little and there was a smile on his mouth. "Science is more powerful than this. It is more powerful than any magic. Its laws are greater laws than magic's laws. Science is more powerful than this."

Some seemed afraid of him then. But most of them were cued by the chief who was arrogant with disdain.

"If science is so great, I would know it. But nothing is greater than magic. I would like to see a thing greater than magic."

"I would be glad to show you," said Angus. He took out a pocket light and turned it on, lighting up the entire hut. But when he shut it off, the sleek youth waved his hand and the hut became twice as light.

The chief laughed. "Is there no more to your science?"

"There is much more," said Angus. "Science can do anything which this young man's magic can do."

There was a titter of disbelief. Sergeant Dirk moved back a pace, the better to wield a morning star of his own manufacture in case the going got rough.

"Magic can drive people mad," said the chief.

"Science can make people sane," said Angus.

"In any contest with magic," suddenly announced the fat young man, grown very proud, "your science would lose."

Angus looked straight across the fire at the round, greasy face of the self-styled magician. "If we were to engage in a contest, I should beat you."

The young man leaped up in triumph. "He has declared it. He has called the challenge and he is the challenger. Behold, I call you all to witness. These people would come upon us and rob and kill us but their science is not great. Here is one who challenges me! I accept the challenge!" He sat down promptly.

The chief smiled and his eyes glittered with a sporting thirst. "You have challenged, newcomer. It shall be arranged. When two warriors of our people disagree, they fight before all. You shall fight against our Taubo, he whom you have challenged. You have your rights. You shall fight."

Angus sighed but he nodded.

"You are aware of our rules?" said the chief.

"I am not," said Angus.

"Then I shall dictate the rules of this contest. Taubo shall have the morning in which to destroy you with his magic. You shall have the afternoon to destroy him with your science. Then so shall it be proved."

Sergeant Dirk tugged at Angus' shoulder. "Pull out, sir. It'll be poison and no chaser. I'll—" He stopped at his boss' quick glance.

Angus thought for a while and poked a coal with the end of his cane. Then he looked at the chief and said, "I accept this 'contest.'" He stood up and bowed to the young man. "I wish you every success," he said ironically and, turning on his heel, left the hut.

The word raced across the gigantic valley and for a week outlanders poured into the center, bringing with them scanty provisions but a voracious curiosity. They came, dragging children and weird animals, to aid in the erection of a brush amphitheater, to gossip all day and dance all night, and to gawp about the *Argus 48* and be kept at a distance by the marines.

The dust was thick, even within the ship, and Angus McBane wore a bandana across the lower part of his face as he read. He had to lift the bandana to sip at a drink and he occasionally had to lift his eyes from print to make some answer to Sergeant Dirk toiling in the room beyond.

Dirk had come into the Marine Corps under sentence never to be seen in civilian clothes again. He had left his right name behind but he had brought his ingenuity. Now and again some glimpse of his past would come up when a job needed to be done. But it was only a glimpse, like a curtain flicked back for an instant upon a long and gore-spattered corridor, and Angus never inquired.

Too tough even for the corps, Dirk had been shunted to Civil Affairs, that catchall for odd men and odder jobs, and under Angus McBane he had managed to keep reasonably out of trouble. This was because he had found in his calloused and sin-choked heart, an affection for the officer. Time and again Angus had raked him out of drunk tanks and sent him back to duty without a tour in the infamous "dancing school" and Dirk, out of continually mounting gratitude, fondly supposed that he had shielded Angus from the facts of life.

When he lifted his eyes, Angus could see the jagged peaks

which bounded the north of the valley and the rolling, dusty, scrub-covered lands which intervened. The place could be fertile, if these people could be coerced into the practices of agriculture. It was a wonder they had not discovered that their hunter society had begun to fail a century or two ago. They practiced infanticide and senicide to keep their population down to near food production level and yet they left untended better than ten thousand square miles of arable land. Such things irked Angus. Professionally, he was supposed to be indifferent to these things. But he was not. They distressed him.

"—so I says to this girl, 'Baby, if it's money that's worryin' you, take a look.' And then I found myself in a gutter with a headache and that's how I come to distrust wimmen," narrated Dirk. "The more sweet and beautiful they appear, the more I distrusts 'em. You got to be careful." He was busy with a small set of cogs which were entirely swallowed in his enormous hands. "Aw, you ain't listenin'."

"Sergeant," said Angus, "we can do a lot for these people."

Dirk looked out the port at the dusty land and the throng of gaping multicolored 'goonies.' He looked at his officer. "If you ast me, a dose of ray would cure 'em best. Sir, they got about as much heart as a Jack Ketch. They revels at the sight of blood and howls in glee at the screams of the dead and dyin'. They're an outlandish and immoral lot of swine!"

"I am sure you are an authority on morals, Sergeant. But the dose of ray you suggest would turn this place into a new nova."

"You kiddin'?"

"I am sure I am not," said Angus.

"Then you better not let Edwards run that guard by hisself. *He* ain't got any sense."

"There isn't a loaded gun on board," said Angus. "And not one round."

Dirk looked through the port at the crowding, jostling humanoids. He looked at the dangling weapons, the filed teeth and the rolling eyes. He swallowed, coughed his chew of tobacco back up and spat in confusion. "That's why the scouts left their dead behind!"

"Right," said Angus. "Here comes the chief."

That dignitary was being carried on a litter of animal skins to the ship. His guards clubbed the crowd away, walked on a body or two and came to a halt at the airlock.

The chief got all seven feet of him to the ground and entered the ship. He was not dismayed by the machinery. You couldn't hunt with it and so it was subject only to contempt.

"Taubo ready in the morning."

"That is a day early," said Angus.

"Taubo ready in the morning," said the chief.

They bowed. The chief got back on his litter and was carried away. The stricken lay where they had fallen, trodden down again by the curious.

"Civilize 'em!" said Dirk. "Give me twenty men and fixed bayonets and I'll civilize 'em. We won't be ready by morning!"

"We will," said Angus, putting the book aside. "Indeed we will."

The brush arena was jammed, presenting a wall of faces and a surge of odors which would have overpowered a lion. Three thousand humanoids had turned out this day to witness Taubo present a display of his powers and to howl over the downfall of the strange invaders. Deltoid had turned Mandrel's light above the rim and the far mountains were washed with pink. The dust had been settled by sprayings of water and pennons hung at either side of the arena.

Taubo came with his assistants. He was a wily young man, Taubo. He had succeeded his teacher and the former head of his profession by a very effective dose of poison and his followers, knowing it well, served him with deference which, while it was not devotion, was at least efficient dignity.

The group toured the arena and then, in the center, Taubo leaped up, flung wide his arms and let loose a dreadful screech. It was a well-practiced screech and it would nearly deafen at five feet. It started high and went higher and it had volume enough to satisfy the most savage. But it had more purpose than mere satisfaction. Many a victim had been paralyzed into complete obedience by that screech.

The crowd was instantly silent.

"I am Taubo!" cried the magician. "I come to show the invader of my power so that he will forever be afraid to come to us again from beyond the mountains. I am Taubo! I drink fresh blood and I dine on newborn children! One sight of my magic and the strongest sicken. One blast of my breath and men die. I am Taubo. My magic protects us from becoming slaves. *I shall conquer!*"

That was most satisfying to them all and, when they had recovered a little from fright, they cheered and cheered, beating wooden lances against hide shields and waving skins in the air.

But this had to end. They expected something very spectacular from the other pennon. A small knot of human beings had been gathered there since the first streaks of dawn. They had a raised curtain and from time to time one or another glanced into it.

Taubo became brave. He capered toward the humans, shouting for them to come forth and let him have his will of them, promising things which were truly blood-laking. Taubo ran back again to the seated chiefs.

"Make them come forth! They are cowards. Make them come! I will strike them where they are if they do not start!"

A chief raised a hand and a horn blew for silence.

"Come forth, invaders!" commanded the chief.

Three thousand pairs of humanoid eyes watched the curtain. It twitched. A form walked forth, calmly, certainly, carrying a chair and a book, and the crowd recognized the leader of the invaders.

The invader's cane was tucked under his arm and he seemed to be neither impressed nor hurried. He put the chair down in the exact center of the arena and sat upon it. He put the cane across his knees and he opened the book. And then calmly, very calmly, he began to scan the pages with a quiet eye.

Taubo leaped forward. He paused only long enough to wave his arms in salute to the crowd and then he went to work.

Coming to within a foot of the invader's ear he let loose a screech which rocked the first rows. It was long, loud and deafening.

The quiet eyes continued to scan the pages.

Taubo let go a howl of disappointment which was not part of his program. He backed up. Then he reached a hand toward a follower and took a wand.

Two of his people began to beat upon a drum and the shocks of it were physical. Close up they were enough to stop a heart, properly directed. Taubo waved the wand. A curtain of fire began to play about the invader's head.

After a few minutes of this, a woman and an old man in the near rows fell out of their seats, insensible.

The drumming continued, grew louder, the whole force of it solidly directed at the breast of the quiet reader. The lightning played and crackled, set fire to a tunic of one of Taubo's followers and had to be put out.

For half an hour the beating continued.

The invader turned pages calmly.

"You Angus!" screamed Taubo. "You wait. I fix you!"

Taubo was becoming angry. He pulled forth an incense pot and he put some coals into it from a fire near his pennon. His followers knew now not to get downwind of that pot. One whiff and a man would die. Taubo dropped some powder into it and blue flames and dense clouds began to roll, clouds which Taubo avoided.

The engulfing smoke bore down upon the seated invader, swallowed him up from sight, drifted across the field and abruptly and with agony killed a wandering dog. It reached the arena edge and a man leaped up and clawed, his throat bleeding. The area of the smoke was hastily cleared.

The charge in the pot sputtered out. Taubo stared.

Another page was being turned!

After a frenzy of rage in which he beat two followers, Taubo came back to his business at hand. He made a number of incantations, driving them home with flashes of light from his wand. He did not expect these would have any effect but they were good showmanship. Then he trotted back and gingerly scooped up a small spade of gray powder. He carefully touched none of it. It was culled from a certain bush and when distilled, a pinch of it on the skin caused an exquisite and rapid dying.

Taubo capered, careful of the powder, and made further loud incantations, interspersed with numerous shrieks and wailings which were orders to the demons of the place to do their worst.

He dashed in suddenly, tipped the spade and showered a cascade of violent poison over his enemy.

Gleeful now, Taubo capered back, expecting an instantaneous effect, since the powder had touched the face and the hands.

The invader tipped the book to clear the print, put the volume back on his knees, and went on reading!

The crowd was becoming a little restless. The sun was rather high now and they had not come to see a magician dance but an invader die. Then, that imperturbable figure was beginning to wear upon them almost as much as it did on Taubo. They had seen magic operate before!

Taubo withdrew. For a long time he took advices with his followers and at last decided upon the final trick.

He had planted, that morning, a number of very tindery bushes underneath the sand and he had saturated them with an oil which burned furiously. He had not thought he would have to use this trick, but the time was at hand.

Taubo marched forth with a loud beating of drums and delivered a wailing chant which again captured his audience. He capered about the reading invader and raced to the points of a star he was drawing on the ground with a wand.

When he had finished a long show of this, he gave an imperceptible signal to a follower and suddenly pointed his wand at a point of the star.

Flame burst.

To the crowd it appeared as though the ground itself was on fire. The smoke rolled and the flames rose pale yellow and smoking in the daylight. At the exact center of the star sat the reader of books.

The fire swept forward, leaped higher. It came to the invader's toes. The drums rolled a heavy, rising storm. The flames went under the invader's feet! Then the smoke was thick and the crowd could not see. But the chair was charring. The entire star was burning in the sand. It was obvious that nothing human could live in that "magic" fire!

Slowly the spent flames died down. The smoke blew aside. Taubo stared.

The invader turned another page!

The entire arena came to its feet with a moan. Taubo started forward. He was becoming red in the face. He had his wand lifted to strike and the shaking tension within tore at him. He moved another step forward, wand still raised. And then he fell, headlong, dead.

If those three thousand humanoids could have moved, they would have done so. They could not. From terror they stood as though tied.

The invader glanced up at the sun, saw that it was overhead and rose from the chair. Finger keeping his place, he walked straight toward the pennons which marked his side. He passed into the curtain and out of sight.

The crowd, chiefs and all, would have run away if Angus had not instantly come out. He marched straight to the bank of notables.

His hair was wet with sweat, his face was black with grime. He stopped and looked at the chiefs.

"You have seen how impervious science is to magic," he said. "I ask you to concede that I have won and that all my demands must therefore be fulfilled. I shall not kill you. I shall help you, for science does not kill, it saves. Do you acknowledge my sovereignty on this planet in the name of the Galactic Council and the Civil Affairs Branch of the Military Defense?"

They took in his words. They realized that he was not that instant going to kill them. And then they looked at the body of Taubo and sensed somehow that they were free of a thing they could not describe.

They looked at Angus McBane with his lank black hair

and his soiled tunic and his cane and suddenly, as the chiefs rose to assent, the humanoids began to cheer. They cheered louder and louder and babies cried and dogs barked, and sound rose in an enthusiasm which was loud enough to be physical force.

"You hear the people," said the high chief. "I hear the people. We acknowledge your science and assent to your rule. You are our lord and your person is sacred unto us forevermore."

Angus bowed and walked back through the swelling din to the curtains and the enclosure.

That evening Angus McBane, Civil Affairs, sent off a laconic dispatch to his superiors.

> DELTOIDS WILL NOT OBJECT TO MINING
> OPERATIONS. EQUIPMENT MAY BE SENT
> AT ANY TIME.
> MCBANE

In the machine shop, meanwhile, of the *Argus 48* Sergeant Dirk finished his careful neutralizing, according to McBane's directions, of the robot McBane had designed and he had built. It was not a very good likeness of McBane anyway, and besides, they needed the parts. McBane regretted the destruction of one perfectly good book.

THE DANGEROUS
DIMENSION

Author's Note

For reasons pertinent to the happiness of Mankind, by request from the United States Philosophic Society and the refusal of Dr. Henry Mudge, Ph.D., of Yamouth University, the philosophic equation mentioned herein is presented as only *Equation C* without further expansion.

—L. Ron Hubbard

THE DANGEROUS DIMENSION

T HE room was neither mean nor dingy. It was only
cluttered. The great bookcases had gaps in their ranks
and the fallen members lay limp-leaved on floor and table.
The carpet was a snowdrift of wasted paper. The stuffed owl
on the mantel was awry because the lined books there had
fallen sideways, knocking the owl around and over to peck
dismally at China on the globe of the world. The writing
desk was heaped with tottering paper towers.

And still Dr. Mudge worked on.

His spectacles worried him because they kept falling down
in front of his eyes; a spot of ink was on his nose and his right
hand was stained blue black.

The world could have exploded without in the least
disturbing Yamouth's philosophic professor. In his head whirled
a maelstrom of philosophy, physics and higher mathematics
and, if examined from within, he would have seemed a very
brave man.

Examined from without it was a different matter. For one
thing Dr. Mudge was thin, for another he was bald. He was
a small man and his head was far too big for his body. His
nose was long and his eyes were unusually bright. His thin
hands gripped book and pen as every atom of his being was
concentrated upon his work.

Once he glanced up at the clock with a worried scowl. It was six-thirty and he must be done in half an hour. He had to be done in half an hour. That would give him just time enough to rush down to the university and address the United States Philosophic Society.

He had not counted on this abrupt stab of mental lightning. He had thought to deliver a calm address on the subject, "Was Spinoza Right in Turning Down the Professorship of . . ." But when he had begun to delve for a key to Spinoza, a truly wonderful idea had struck him and out he had sailed, at two that day, to dwell wholly in thought. He did not even know that he was cramped from sitting so long in one place.

"Henrrreeee!" came the clarion call.

Henry failed to hear it.

"HENrrrry!"

Again he did not look up.

"HENRY MUDGE! Are you going to come in here and eat your dinner or not?!"

He heard that time, but with less than half an ear. He did not come fully back to the world of beefsteak and mashed potatoes until Mrs. Doolin, his housekeeper, stood like a thundercloud in the study door. She was a big woman with what might be described as a forceful personality. She was very righteous, and when she saw the state of that study she drew herself up something on the order of a general about to order an execution.

"Henry! What have you been doing? And look at you! A smudge on your nose—and *an ink spot on your coat!*"

Henry might fight the universe, but Mrs. Doolin was the

76

bogeyman of Henry's life. Ten years before, she had descended upon him and since that time . . .

"Yes, Lizzie," said Henry, aware for the first time of his stiffness and suddenly very tired.

"Are you coming to dinner or aren't you? I called you a half-hour ago and the beefsteak will be ruined. And you must dress. What on earth's gotten into you, Henry Mudge?"

"Yes, Lizzie," said the doctor placatingly. He came slowly to his feet and his joints cracked loudly.

"What *have* you done to this place?"

Some of the fire of his enthusiasm swept back into Henry. "Lizzie, I think I have it!" And that thought swept even Lizzie Doolin out of the room as far as he was concerned. He took a few excited steps around the table, raised his glasses up on his forehead and gleamed. "I think I've got it!"

"What?" demanded Lizzie Doolin.

"The equation. Oh, this is wonderful. This is marvelous! Lizzie, if I am right, there is a condition without dimension. A negative dimension, Lizzie. Think of it! And all these years they have been trying to find the fourth positive dimension and now by working backwards . . ."

"Henry Mudge, what *are* you talking about?"

But Henry had dived into the abstract again and the lightning was flashing inside his head. "The negative dimension! Epistemology!"

"What?"

He scarcely knew she was there. "Look, think of it! You know what you can do with your mind. Mentally you can think you are in Paris. *Zip,* your mind has mentally taken you

77

to Paris! You can imagine yourself swimming in a river and *zip!* you are mentally swimming in a river. But the body stays where it is. And why, Lizzie? *Why?*"

"Henry Mudge—!"

"But there is a negative dimension. I am sure there is. I have almost formulated it and if I can succeed—"

"Henry Mudge, your dinner is getting cold. Stop this nonsense. . . ."

But he had not heard her. Suddenly he gripped his pen and wrote. And on that blotted piece of paper was set down Equation C.

He was not even aware of any change in him. But half his brain began to stir like an uneasy beast. And then the other half began to stir and mutter.

And on the sheet before him was Equation C.

"Henry Mudge!" said Lizzie with great asperity. "If you don't come in here and eat your dinner this very minute . . ." She advanced upon him as the elephant moves upon the dog.

Henry knew in that instant that he had gone too far with her. And half his brain recognized the danger in her. For years he had been in deadly terror of her. . . .

"I wish I was in Paris," Henry shivered to himself, starting to back up.

Whup!

Cognac, m'sieu?" said the waiter.

"Eh?" gaped Henry, glancing up from the sidewalk table. He could not take it in. People were hurrying along the *Rue de la Paix,* going home as the hour was very late. Some of the cafés were already closed.

"*Cognac o vin blanc, m'sieu?*" insisted the waiter.

"Really," said Henry, "I don't drink. I—Is this Paris?"

"Of a certainty, *m'sieu.* Perhaps one has already had a sip too much?"

"No, no! I don't drink," said Henry, frightened to be in such a position.

The waiter began to count the saucers on the table. "Then *m'sieu* has done well for one who does not drink. Forty francs, *m'sieu.*"

Henry guiltily reached into his pocket. But his ink-stained jacket was not his street coat. He had carpet slippers on his feet. His glasses fell down over his eyes. And his searching hands told him that he possessed not a dime.

"Please," said Henry, "I am out of funds. If you would let me—"

"SO!" cried the waiter, suavity vanishing. "Then you will pay just the same! *GENDARME! GENDARME!*"

"Oh," shivered Henry and imagined himself in the peaceful security of his study.

Whup!

Lizzie was gaping at him. "Why . . . why, where . . . where did you go? Oh, it must be my eyes. I know it must be my eyes. Those fainting spells did mean something then. Yes, I am sure of it." She glanced at the clock. "Look, you haven't eaten dinner yet! You come right into the dining room this instant!"

Meekly, but inwardly aghast, Henry tagged her into the dining room. She set a plate before him. He was not very hungry, but he managed to eat. He was greatly perplexed and upset. The negative dimension had been there after all. And there was certainly no difficulty stepping into it and out of it. Mind was everything, then, and body nothing. Or mind could control body. . . . Oh, it was very puzzling.

"What are you dreaming about?" challenged Lizzie. "Get upstairs and get dressed. It's seven this very minute!"

Henry plodded out into the hall and up the stairs. He got to his room and saw that all his things were laid out.

Oh, it was very puzzling, he told himself as he sat down on the edge of the bed. He started to remove one carpet slipper and then scowled in deep thought at the floor.

Twenty minutes later Lizzie knocked at his door. "Henry, you're late already!"

He started guiltily. He had not even taken that slipper off. If Lizzie found him in here— She was starting to open the door.

"I ought to be there this very minute," thought Henry, envisioning the lecture hall.

Whup!

It startled him to see them filing in. He stood nervously on the platform, suddenly aware of his carpet slippers and ink-stained working jacket, the spot on his nose and his almost black hand. Nervously, he tried to edge back.

The dean was there. "Why . . . why, Dr. Mudge. I didn't see you come in." The dean looked him up and down and frowned. "I hardly think that your present attire . . . "

Henry visualized the clothes laid out on his bed and started to cough an apology.

"I . . . er . . ."

Whup!

What's that, Henry?" said Lizzie. "My heavens, where are you?"

"In here, Lizzie," said Henry on the edge of his bed.

She bustled into the room. "Why, you're not dressed! Henry Mudge, I don't know what is happening to your wits. You will keep everybody waiting at the university—"

"Ohhh," groaned Henry. But it was too late.

Whup!

My dear fellow," said the dean, startled. "What . . . er . . . what happened to you? I was saying that I scarcely thought it proper—"

"Please, I—" But that was as far as Henry got.

Whup!

I know it's my eyes," said Lizzie.

"Stop!" wailed Henry. "Don't say anything! Please don't say anything. Please, please, please don't say anything!"

She was suddenly all concern. "Why, you're pale, Henry. Don't you feel well?"

"No—I mean yes. I'm all right. But don't suggest anything. I . . ." But how could he state it? He was frightened half to death by the sudden possibilities which presented themselves to him. All he had to do was visualize anything and that scene

81

was the scene in which he found himself. All anybody had to do was suggest something and *zip!* there he was.

At first it had been a little difficult, but the gigantic beast Thought had risen into full power.

"You dress," said Lizzie.

But he was afraid to start disrobing. What if he thought—

No, he must learn to control this. Somehow he had missed something. If he could get the entire equation straight and its solution, he would have the full answer. But Thought was drunk with power and would not be denied.

Henry rushed past Mrs. Doolin and down the steps to his study. He quickly sat in his chair and gripped his pen with determination. There was Equation C. Now if he could solve the rest of it he would be all right. He only had to substitute certain values . . .

Lizzie had followed him down. "Henry, I think you must be going crazy. Imagine keeping all those men waiting in the lecture hall—"

Whup!

Henry groaned and heard the dean say, "It was to be our pleasure this evening that we hear from Dr. Mudge on the subject—"

Somebody twitched at the dean's sleeve. "He's right beside you."

The dean looked and there was Henry, tweed jacket, ink stains, carpet slippers and all. Beads of perspiration were standing out on Henry's bulging forehead.

"Go right ahead," whispered the dean. "I do not approve of your attire, but it is too late now."

Henry stood up, fiery red and choked with stage fright. He looked down across the amused sea of faces and cleared his throat. The hall quieted slowly.

"Gentlemen," said Henry, "I have made a most alarming discovery. Forgive me for so appearing before you, but it could not be helped. Mankind has long expected the existence of a state of mind wherein it might be possible to follow thought. However—" His lecture presence broke as he recalled his carpet slippers. Voice nervous and key-jumpy, he rushed on. "However, the arrival at actual transposition of person by thought alone was never attained because mankind has been searching forward instead of backward. That is, mankind has been looking for the existence of nothing in the fourth dimension instead of the existence—" He tried to make his mind clear. Stage fright was making him become involved. "I mean to say, the negative dimension is not the fourth dimension but no dimension. The existence of nothing as . . ."

Some of the staid gentlemen in the front row were not so staid. They were trying not to laugh because the rest of the hall was silent.

"What idiocy is that man babbling?" said the dean to the university president behind his hand.

Dr. Mudge's knees were shaking. Somebody tittered openly in the fourth row.

"I mean," plunged Mudge, desperately, "that when a man imagines himself elsewhere, his mind seems to really be elsewhere for the moment. The yogi takes several means of accomplishing this, evidently long practiced in the negative dimension. Several great thinkers such as Buddha have been able to appear bodily at a distance when they weren't there but . . ." he swallowed again, "but elsewhere when they were there. The metaphysicist has attributed supernatural qualities to the phenomenon known as an 'apport,' in which people and such appear in one room without going through a door when they were in the other room. . . ."

Dear me, he thought to himself, this is a dreadful muddle. He could feel the truth behind his words, but he was too acutely aware of a stained jacket and carpet slippers and he kept propping up his glasses.

"If a man should wish to be in some other place, it is entirely possible for him to imagine himself in that place, and, diving back through the negative dimension, to emerge out of it in that place with instantaneous rapidity. To imagine oneself—"

He swallowed hard. An awful thought had hit him, big enough to make him forget his clothes and audience. A man could imagine himself anyplace and then be in that place, *zip*! But how could a man exert enough willpower to keep from imagining himself in a position of imminent destruction? If he thought— Mudge gritted his teeth. He must not think any such thing. He must *not*! He knew instinctively that there was one place he could not imagine himself without dying instantly before he could recover and retreat. He did not know the name of that place in the instant, would not allow himself to think of it—

A ribald young associate professor said hoarsely to a friend, loud enough for Dr. Mudge to hear, "He ought to imagine himself on Mars."

Mudge didn't even hear the laugh which started to greet that sally.

Whup!

He examined the sandy wastes which stretched limitlessly to all the clear horizons. Bewildered, he took a few steps and the sand got into his carpet slippers. A cold wind cut through the thin tweed jacket and rustled his tie.

"Oh, dear," thought Mudge. "Now I've done it!"

A high, whining sound filled the sky and he glanced up to see a pear-shaped ship streaking flame across the sky. It was gone almost before it had started.

Dr. Mudge felt very much alone. He had no faith in his mental behavior now. It might fail him. He might never get away. He might imagine himself in an emperor's palace with sentries—

Whup!

The diamond floor was hard on his eyes and lights blazed all around him. A golden throne reared before him and on top of it sat a small man with a very large head, swathed in material which glowed all of itself.

Mudge couldn't understand a word that was being said because no words were being said, and yet they all hit his brain in a bewildering disarray.

*The diamond floor was hard on his eyes and lights blazed
all around him. A golden throne reared before him and
on top of it sat a small man with a very large head,
swathed in material which glowed all of itself.*

Instantly he guessed what was happening. As a man's intention can be telepathed to a dog, these superior beings battered him mentally as he had no brain wave selectivity. He had guessed the human mind would so evolve, and he was pleased for an instant to find he had been right. But not for long.

He began to feel sick in the midst of this bombardment. All eyes were upon him in frozen surprise.

The emperor shouted and pointed a small wand. Two guards leaped up and fastened themselves upon Mudge. He knew vaguely that they thought he was an inferior being—something like a chimpanzee, or maybe a gorilla, and, indeed, so he was on their scale of evolution.

The ruler shouted again and the guards breathed hard and looked angrily at Mudge. Another man came sprinting over the diamond floor, a flare-barreled gun gripped in his hand.

Mudge began to struggle. He knocked the guards aside with surprising ease.

Wildly he turned about, seeking a way out, too confused by light, thought waves and sound to think clearly and remember.

The man with the lethal-looking weapon braced his feet and leveled the muzzle at Mudge's chest. He was going to shoot and Mudge knew that he faced a death-dealing ray. He was getting no more consideration than a mad ape, like that one in the Central Park Zoo. . . . The guard was squeezing the trigger—

Whup!

Weakly Dr. Mudge leaned on the railing of the Central Park Zoo in New York. He took out his handkerchief and dabbed at his forehead. Dully he gazed up, knowing he would see an orangutan in the cage. It was late, and the beast slumbered in his covered hut. Mudge could only see a tuft of fur.

"Thanks," he whispered.

The night air was soothing. He was exhausted with all the crosscurrents which had battered his poor human mind, and the thin air of Mars.

He moved slowly along the rail. There was a sign there which said "Gorilla. Brought from the Mountains of the Moon by Martin—"

Whup!

Ohhh," groaned Mudge pitifully as he sank down on a rock in the freezing night. "This can't keep up. I would no more than start to eat when something would yank me away. I'd starve. And sooner or later I'll think of a very dangerous place and that will be the end of me before I can escape. There's one place in particular—

"NO!" he screamed into the African night.

The thought had not formed. One place he must never, never think about. NEVER!

From this high peak, he could see all Africa spread before him. Glowing far off in the brilliant moonlight was Lake Tanganyika.

Mudge was a little pleased with himself just the same. Back at the lecture—

Whup!

I am sorry and very puzzled," the dean was saying, watch in hand. "Why Dr. Mudge should see fit to use a magician's tricks, to appear in such strange attire and generally disport himself—"

"I can't help it!" wailed Mudge at his side.

The dean almost jumped out of his shoes. He was annoyed to be startled out of his dignity and he scowled harshly at Mudge. "Doctor, I advise you strongly that such conduct will no longer be tolerated. If you are trying to prove anything by this, an explanation will be most welcome. The subject is philosophy and *not* Houdini's vanishing tricks."

"Ohhh," moaned Mudge, "don't say anything. Please don't say anything more. Just keep quiet. I mean," he said hastily, "I mean, don't say anything else. Please!"

The young man who had suggested Mars was not quite so sure of himself, but the dean's handy explanation of magic without paraphernalia restored his buoyancy.

"I was just . . ." began Mudge. "No, I can't say where I was or I'll go back, and I won't go back. This is very terrifying to me, gentlemen. There is one certain place I must not think about. The mind is an unruly thing. It seems to have no great love for the material body as it willfully, so it seems, insists in this great emergency on playing me tricks—"

"Dr. Mudge," said the dean, sternly. "I know not what you mean by all this cheap pretension to impossibilities—"

"Oh, no," cried Mudge. "I am pretending nothing. If I could only stop this I would be a very happy man! It is terribly hard on the nerves. Out of Spinoza I wandered into Force equations, and at two today I caught a glimmer of truth in the fact that there was a negative dimension—a dimension which had no dimensions. I know for certain that mind is capable of anything."

"It certainly is," said the dean. "Even chicanery."

"No, no," begged Mudge, pushing his glasses high on his forehead and then fishing in his pockets. "In my notes . . ." He looked squarely at the dean. "Here! I have proof of where I have been, sir." He stooped over and took off a carpet slipper. He turned it upside down on the lecture table and a peculiar glowing sand streamed out.

"That is Martian sand," said Mudge.

"BOSH!" cried the dean. He turned to the audience. "Gentlemen, I wish you to excuse this display. Dr. Mudge has not been well and his mind seems to be unbalanced. A few hour's rest—"

"I'll show you my notes," said Mudge, pleading. "I'll show you the equation. I left them home in my study—"

Whup!

Lizzie Doolin was muttering to herself as she picked up the papers from the floor and stacked them. The professor was certainly a madman this evening. Poor little man— She was turning and she almost fainted.

Dr. Mudge was sitting in his chair getting his notes together.

"Doctor!" cried Lizzie. "What are you doing there? How did you get in the house? The doors are all locked and . . . Ohhhhh, it's my eyes. Doctor, you know very well that you should be at that lecture—"

He barely had time to cram the papers in his pocket.
Whup!

The dean was fuming. "Such tricks are known— Oh, there you are! Doctor, I am getting very sick of this. We are too well versed in what can be done by trickery to be at all startled by these comings and goings of yours."

"It's *not* a trick!" stated Mudge. "Look, I have my notes. I—"

"And I suppose you've brought back some vacuum from the moon this—"

Whup!

It was so cold that Mudge was instantly blue all over. He could feel himself starting to blow up as the internal pressure fought for release. His lungs began to collapse, but his mind raced, torn between two thoughts.

Here he was on the moon. Here he was, the first man ever to be on the moon!

And all the great volcanoes reared chilly before him, and an empty Sea of Dreams fell away behind him. Barren rock was harsh beneath his feet and his weight was nothing. . . .

All in an instant he glimpsed it because he knew that he would be dead in another second, exploded like a penny balloon. He visualized the thing best known to him—his study.

Whup!

Lizzie was going out the door when she heard the chair creak. She forgot about the necessity for aspirin as she faced about.

Mudge was in again.

"Doctor," stormed Lizzie, an amazon of fury, "if you don't stop that, I don't know what will happen to me! Here a minute, gone again, here and gone, here and gone! What is the world coming to! It is *not* my eyes. It can't be my eyes. I felt over the whole room for you and not so much as a hair of your head was here. What kind of heathen magic have you been stirring up? You've sold your soul—"

"STOP!" screamed Mudge. He sank back, panting. That had been close. But then, that had not been as close as that other THING which he dared *not* envision. He chopped the thought off and started back on another.

"Maybe," said Mudge, thoughtfully, "maybe there isn't . . . Oh, I've got the test right here. Can I throw myself back and forth between life and death?"

He had said the word.

"Death," he said again, more distinctly.

And still nothing occurred. He breathed easier. He could not go back and forth through time, as he had no disconnection with the time stream. He could whisk himself about the universe at will—or against his will—but he was still carrying on in the same hours and minutes. It had been dark in Africa, almost morning in P—

"NO!" he yelled.

Lizzie jumped a foot and stared to see if Mudge was still in his chair.

"Whatever are you up to?" demanded Lizzie, angrily. "You frighten a body out of her wits!"

"Something awful is going on," said Mudge, darkly. "I tried to tell you before dinner, but you wouldn't listen. I can imagine I am someplace and then be in that someplace. This very instant I could imagine something and *zip*! I'd be someplace else without walking through doors or anything."

Lizzie almost broke forth anew. But it awed her, a little. She had seen Mudge appear and disappear so often this evening that this was the only explanation which she could fit.

Mudge looked tired. "But I'm afraid, Lizzie. I'm terribly afraid. If I don't watch myself, I might imagine I was in some horrible place such as—

"NO!" shouted Mudge.

"I might imagine I was someplace where I—

"NO!" he yelled again.

Those shouts were like bullets to Lizzie Doolin. But she was still awed—a little.

Mudge held his head in his hands. "And I'm in trouble. The dean will not believe what is happening to me. He calls me a cheat—

"NO!" he cried.

"What do you keep yelling for?" complained Lizzie.

"So I won't go sailing off. If I can catch a thought before it forms I can stay put." He groaned and lowered his head into his hands. "But I am not believed. They think me a cheat. Oh, Lizzie, I'll lose my professorship. We'll starve!"

She was touched and advanced slowly to touch his shoulder. "Never you mind what they say about you. I'll beat their heads in, Henry, that I will."

He glanced up in astonishment at her. She had never shown any feeling for him in all these ten years. She had bullied him and driven him and terrified him. . . .

She was conscious of her tenderness and brushed it away on the instant. "But don't go jumping off like that again! Drive over to the university in your car like a decent man should."

"Yes, Lizzie."

He got up and walked toward the door. Her jaw was set again.

"Mind what I tell you," she snapped. "Your car, now! And nothing fancy!"

"Yes, Lizzie. They're waiting. . . ." He didn't, couldn't stop that thought and the hall was clearly envisioned and there he was—

Whup!

The dean had his hands on both hips as he saw that Mudge was here again. The dean wagged his head from side to side and was very angry, almost speechless. The audience tittered.

"Have you no respect?" cried the dean. "How dare you do such things when I am talking to you. I was saying that the next time you'll probably—"

"SHUT UP!" shouted Mudge in desperation. He was still cold from his trip to the moon.

The dean recoiled. Mudge was a very mild little fellow, with never anything but groveling respect for everybody. And these words from him . . .

"I'm sorry," said Mudge. "You mustn't say things or you'll send me off somewhere again. Now don't speak."

"Mudge, you can be assured that this performance this evening will terminate—"

Mudge was desperate. "Don't. You might say something."

The audience was delighted and laughter rolled through the hall. Mudge had not realized how his remark would sound.

The dean had never been anything but overbearing and now with his dignity flouted he turned white. He stepped stiffly to the president of the university and said a few words in a low voice. Grimly the president nodded.

"Here and now," said the dean, stepping back, "I am requesting your resignation, Mudge. This buffoonery—"

"Wait," pleaded Mudge, hauling his notes from his pocket. "First look at these and maybe you will see—"

"I care to look at nothing," stated the dean frostily. "You are a disgrace."

"Look," pleaded Mudge, putting the papers on the lecture stand. "Just give me one minute. I am beside myself. I don't mean what I say. But there is one thing I must not think about—one thing I can't think to think about but which I— Look. Here, see?"

The dean scowled at the sheets of scribbled figures and symbols. Mudge talked to him in a low voice, growing more and more excited.

The dean was still austere.

"And there," said Mudge, "right there is Equation C. Read it."

The dean thought Mudge might as well be humored as long as he would be leaving in the morning for good. He adjusted his glasses and looked at Mudge's reports. His glance fastened on Equation C.

The dean was startled. He stood up straight, his logical mind turning over at an amazing pace. "That's very strange," said the dean, bewildered. "My head feels . . ."

"Oh, what have I done?" cried Mudge, too late.

The assistant professor in the front row, a man of little wit but many jokes, chortled, "I suppose *he* will go to Mars now."

Whup!

Whup!

Mudge was almost in control by now. He knew that a part of Equation C was missing which would make it completely workable and usable at all times without any danger. And he also knew that being here on this sandy plain was not very dangerous unless one happened to think—

"NO!" he screamed into the Martian night.

It was easy. All he had to do was visualize the classroom—

Whup!

Mudge took off his glasses and wiped them. Then he bent over and emptied the sand from his slippers. The hall before him was silent as death and men were staring in disbelief at the little man on the platform.

Mudge replaced the slipper. He took up a pencil and bent eagerly over his notes. He had to work this thing out before he imagined—

"NO!" he roared.

It would be awful if he dreamed it. Dreaming, he would have no real control and things would happen to him.

The president rose cautiously and tapped Mudge's shoulder. "W-W-Where is the dean?"

Mudge glanced around. True enough, the dean was not there. Mudge chewed at the end of his pencil in amazed contemplation.

"Do you mean," ventured the president, "that that statement about—"

"SHUT UP!" cried Mudge. "The dean may find out how to get back unless he thinks of something he . . ." He swallowed hard.

"Dr. Mudge, I resent such a tone," began the president.

"I am sorry," said Mudge, "but you might have said it, and the next time I might fall in a Martian canal—"

Whup!

He was strangling as he fought through the depths. He broke the surface like a porpoise and swam as hard as he could, terror surging within him as these dark waters lapped over him.

Ahead he could see a houseboat with a beautiful lady sitting at the rail. He swam breast stroke, raising himself up to shout for help. The cold suddenness of the accident had dulled his brain and he could not know what monsters lurked in these Martian depths.

The woman was strangely like an Earthwoman for all that. Perhaps there were colonies of these people much as there were colonies of chimpanzees on Earth. But the houseboat was silvery and the woman dressed in luminous cloth.

Strong hands yanked Mudge from the water and he stood

blowing upon the deck, water forming about his feet in a pool. The woman was staring at him. She was a beautiful thing and Mudge's heart beat swiftly. She spoke in sibilant tones.

He bowed to her. "No, I haven't time for a visit or tea or anything," said Mudge. "I am sorry, but I am busy at a lect— NO! I am busy on Ea— NO! I am busy."

Oddly enough he knew that he could not speak her language, and yet he understood her perfectly as she placed her hand on his arm. It must be more telepathy, he thought.

"Yes, it is telepathy," said her mind. "Of course. But I am astonished to see you. For years—ever since the great purge—no humans of our breed have been here. Alone with these yellow men as servants I am safe enough. My parole was given because of certain favors—"

"Please," said Mudge. "I have an appointment. Don't be alarmed if I vanish. I'll be back someday." He looked around to fix the spot in his mind, feeling devilish for an instant.

He bowed to her. "I must leave—"

"But you'll take cold," she said, picking up a shawl of glowing material and throwing it about his shoulders.

"Thank you," said Mudge, "and now I really must go."

Again he bowed, and envisioned the classroom this time. *Whup!*

The water dripped to the lecture platform and Mudge was really getting cold by now. He hauled the shawl more tightly about his arms and was aware of protruding eyes all through the hall.

The water dripped and dripped, and Mudge shivered again. He sneezed. It would be good—

"NO!" he shouted and everybody in the hall jumped almost out of their chairs.

Mudge turned to the president. "You see what you did?"

The president was cowed. But he picked up in a moment. "Did . . . did you see the dean?"

"No," said Mudge. The warm room was drying his clothes rapidly, and he rolled up his sleeve so that he wouldn't blot the paper. Feverishly, he began to evolve Equation D.

He almost knew why he was working so fast. He was wholly oblivious of the audience. Very well he knew that his life depended upon his solving Equation D and thus putting the negative dimension wholly in his control. His pencil flew.

The thought began to seep into his mind in spite of all he could do.

"NO!" he yelled.

Again people jumped.

There was a grunt at his elbow and there stood the dean. He had sand in his gray hair and he looked mussed up.

"So you got back," said Mudge.

"It . . . it was terrible," moaned the dean in a broken voice. "The—"

"Don't say it," said Mudge.

"Doctor," said the dean, "I apologize for all I said to you." He faced the crowd. "I can verify amply everything that has happened here tonight. Dr. Mudge is absolutely correct"—he paused to swab his face and spit sand out of his teeth—"about

99

the negative dimension. I have the uneasy feeling, however, that it is a very dangerous dimension. A man might—"

"Stop!" said Mudge, loudly.

He was working at a terrific pace now, and the paper shot off the stand to the floor as he swept it aside. He grabbed a new sheet.

He knew he was working against death. Knew it with all his heart. That thought would not long be stayed. At any minute he might find out where he was that he dared never go—

Equation D was suddenly before him. He copied it with a weary sigh and handed it to the dean. "Read that before you get any ideas," said Mudge.

The dean read it.

"Mars," said Mudge.

Nothing happened.

The dean began to breathe more easily.

"Moon," said Mudge.

And still nothing happened.

Mudge faced the audience. "Gentlemen, I regret the excitement here tonight. It has quite exhausted me. I can either give you Equation C and D or—"

"No," said the dean.

"NO!" chorused the crowd.

"I'm frightened of it," said the dean. "I could never, never, never prevail upon myself to use it under any circumstances less than a falling building. Destroy it."

Mudge looked around and everybody nodded.

"I know this," said Mudge, "but I will never write it again."

And so saying, he tore it up into little bits, his wet coat making it possible for him to wad the scraps to nothingness, never again to be read by mortal man.

"Gentlemen," said Mudge, "I am chilly. And so if you will excuse me, I will envision my study and—"

Whup!

Lizzie was crying. Her big shoulders shook as she hunched over in the doctor's chair. "Oh, I just know something will happen to him. Something awful," said Lizzie. "Poor little man."

"I am not a poor little man," said Mudge.

She gasped as she stared up at him.

"My chair, please," said Mudge.

She started to her feet. "Why, Henry Mudge, you are soaking wet! What do you mean—?"

He cut her short. "I don't mean anything by it except that I fell in a Martian canal, Lizzie. Now be quick and get me some dry clothes and a drink of something."

She hesitated. "You know you don't drink," she snapped—for a test.

"I don't drink because I knew you didn't like it. Bring me some of that medicinal whiskey, Lizzie. Tomorrow I'll make it a point to get some good Scotch."

"HENRY!"

"Don't talk like that," said Henry Mudge commandingly. "I am warning you that you had better be pretty good from now on."

"Henry," said Lizzie.

"Stop that," he said. "I won't have it. I refuse to be bullied in my own home, I tell you. And unless you are very, very good I am liable to vanish like that—"

"Don't," she begged. "Don't do that, Henry. Please don't do that. Anything you say, Henry. Anything. But don't pop off like that anymore."

Henry beamed upon her. "That's better. Now go get me some clothes and a drink. And be quick about it."

"Yes, Henry," she said meekly. But even so she did not feel badly about it. In fact, she felt very good. She whisked herself upstairs and trotted down again in a moment.

She placed the whiskey and water beside his hand.

Henry dug up a forbidden cigar. She did not protest.

"Get me a light," said Henry.

She got him a light. "If you want anything, dear, just call."

"That I will, Lizzie," said Henry Mudge.

He put his feet upon the desk, feeling wicked about it but enjoying it just the same. His clothes were almost dry.

He sank back puffing his cigar, and then took a sip of the drink. He chuckled to himself.

His mind had quieted down. He grinned at the upset owl. The thought which had almost hit him before came to him now. It jarred him for an instant, even made him sweat. But he shook it off and was very brave.

"Sun," said Henry Mudge, coolly taking another drink.

STORY PREVIEW

STORY PREVIEW

N OW that you've just ventured through some of the captivating tales in the Stories from the Golden Age collection by L. Ron Hubbard, turn the page and enjoy a preview of *A Matter of Matter*. Join Chuck Lambert, who is not exactly a fool, but who is guilty of letting his imagination get the best of his wits. Enter an unsavory real estate swindler of a galactic economy, who can commit larceny on a stupendous scale: he sells unwary customers a planet where they can't sit down, because there's something the matter with its matter. And that's exactly what becomes the matter for our unlucky voyager, after Chuck innocently buys a planet of his own.

A Matter of Matter

YOU have seen the gaudy little shops along Broadway. Well, this is a warning not to patronize them.

Planets can be bought perfectly legally from the Interior Department of the Outer Galactic Control and you don't have to follow up the ads you read and hear over the radio; for no matter what they say, there is many a man who would be in much better health today if he had not succumbed to:

IT'S A POOR MAN
WHO ISN'T KING
IN SOME CORNER.
EMPIRES FOR A PITTANCE.
THRONES FOR A MITE.

Easy Payments, Nothing Down.
Honest Mike

It sounds so simple, it is so simple. Who would not be an Earthman in this vital day? But who would be a fool?

Chuck Lambert was not exactly a fool. He was top-heavy. He let his imagination sweep away all such things as petty logic, shaped up the facts into something which satisfied his dreams and went merrily along, auto-blinded to anything which shadowed what he wanted to believe. Lady Luck, that mischievous character, is sometimes patient with a fool—and sometimes she loads with buckshot and lets him have it.

When he was eighteen Chuck Lambert, having precociously finished college, got a job moving packing cases and found, after six months of it, that his boss, a septuagenarian named Coley, received exactly three dollars a day more than Chuck and had had to wait forty years for his advancement. This was a blow. Chuck had visions of being president of the company at the age of twenty-four until he discovered this. The president was taking some glandular series or other and was already ninety and would live another hundred years.

Discouragement lasted just long enough to call Chuck's attention to Madman Murphy, the King of Planetary Realtors, whose magnificent display, smooth conversation, personal pounciness and assumption that Chuck had decided before he had closed a deal, opened wide the gates to glory.

Chuck was to work hard and invest every dime he could scrape into Project 19453X. This included, when it would at last be paid for, a full and clear deed of title, properly recorded and inviolate to the end of time to heirs and assigns forever, to the Planet 19453X. Murphy threw in as the clincher, free rental of a Star-Jumper IV and all supplies for the initial trip.

When he was out on the sidewalk, Chuck suddenly realized that it was going to take him eleven years of very hard work to pay for that planet, providing he starved himself the while and had no dates, and he went back in to reason with Madman Murphy.

"Look, Mr. Murphy, it stands to reason that all these

minerals and things are worth a lot more than the price. I'm more valuable *on* that planet than I am here working as a clerk. Now what I propose—"

"Young man, I congratulate you!" said Murphy. "I envy your youth and prospects! Godspeed and bless you!" And he answered the phone.

An aide took Chuck back to the walk and let him reel home on his own steam. He couldn't afford, now, an airlift. He had eleven long years before him when he couldn't afford one. He was perfectly free to walk unless his shoes wore out—no provision having been made to replace them in this budget of eighty percent of pay. He was particularly cheered when the aide said, "Just to stiffen your resolution, and for no other reason than because Madman Murphy really likes you, you understand that this is no provisional contract. If you don't pay, we garnishee your pay for the period and keep the planet, too. That's the law and we're sorry for it. Now, God bless you and goodbye."

Chuck didn't need blessings as much as he needed help. It was going to be a very long and gruesome servitude.

As the months drifted off the calendar and became years, Chuck Lambert still had his literature to console him but nothing else. It is no wonder that he became a little lopsided about Planet 19453X.

He had a brochure which had one photograph in it and a mimeographed sheet full of adjectives, and if the photograph was not definitely of his planet and if the adjectives did not add into anything specific, they cheered him in his drudgery.

Earth, at this time, had a million or more planets at its disposal, several hundred thousand of them habitable and only a hundred and fifty colonized. The total revenue derived by Earth from these odds and ends of astronomy was not from the colonies but from the sale of land to colonists. The normal price of land on New World, being about one and one-half cents an acre, was a fair average price for all properly colonized planets. Unsurveyed orbs, nebulously labeled "Believed habitable," were scattered over the star charts like wheat in a granary.

On the normal, colonized planet, Earth's various companies maintained "stations" where supplies, a doctor and a government of sorts were available. On Planet 19453X there would be no doctor, no supplies, and no government except Chuck Lambert.

He realized this in his interminable evenings when he sat, dateless, surrounded by technical books, atlases and dirty teacups. The more he read of the difficulties overcome by the early colonizers on warrantedly habitable planets, the thinner his own project began to seem.

He would cheer himself at these times by the thought that the whole thing was only costing him twenty-five thousand dollars and blind himself to the fact that better-known bargains often went for two hundred fifty dollars on the government auction block. Chuck was top-heavy with imagination. He let it be his entire compass.

At the end of three years he had made a great deal of progress. The librarian had come to know him. She was a pleasant young thing who had her own share of imagination—and troubles—and it gave her pleasure to dredge up new books for Chuck to imbibe. Her guidance—her name was Isabel—and his voracity put him through medicine by the time four years had passed, electronics by five and a half, geology by six, mineralogy by seven, government theory by seven and a quarter, space navigation by eight, surveying by nine, and all the rest of the odds and ends by eleven.

She was rather good-looking, and when she had finally lost her first, elementary desire to marry a millionaire, she began to understand that she was in love with Chuck. After all, when you spend eleven years helping an ambitious young man to plow through a dream, you are likely to be interested in him.

She would have gone with him without another thought if he had asked her. But his last visit to the library was a very formal one. He was carrying a bouquet and he said a little speech.

"Isabel, I hope some day to prove a worthy investment of your time. I hope to be able to bring you a three-headed butler or maybe a dog in a matchbox to show my appreciation of your interest. Tomorrow I am faring forth. Goodbye."

To find out more about *A Matter of Matter* and how you can obtain your copy, go to www.goldenagestories.com.

GLOSSARY

GLOSSARY

STORIES FROM THE GOLDEN AGE *reflect the words and expressions used in the 1930s and 1940s, adding unique flavor and authenticity to the tales. While a character's speech may often reflect regional origins, it also can convey attitudes common in the day. So that readers can better grasp such cultural and historical terms, uncommon words or expressions of the era, the following glossary has been provided.*

Aldrich Deep: *deeps* are areas of the ocean over 3,000 fathoms (18,000 feet) deep. The Aldrich Deep, located east of New Zealand and nearly the size of Australia, is one of the largest and is named after Admiral Pelham Aldrich who measured its depth in the 1800s. The Aldrich Deep has been measured at 5,155 fathoms (30,930 feet).

auto-blinded: to have made oneself unable to notice or understand something.

blood-laking: causing blood to pool in the lower parts of the body, thus denying blood to the brain, often resulting in a person fainting or passing out. Blood-laking can be triggered by fear, bad news or unpleasant sights, the resultant shock creates a sudden nervous system reaction that produces temporary dilation of blood vessels, reducing the blood supply to the brain.

CA: Civil Affairs.

catalyst crystals: crystals or minerals that cause or accelerate a chemical reaction without themselves being affected.

city room: the room in which local news is handled for a newspaper, a radio station or for another journalistic agency.

crackbrain: a foolish, senseless or insane person.

cub: cub reporter; a young and rather inexperienced newspaper reporter.

"dancing school": another name for a brothel.

dissolution of Gaul: "Pop chose to attempt the dissolution of Gaul in the manufactures of Kentucky" is a play on words, meaning that he tried to drown his bitter feelings in whiskey. The two words are *Gaul* and *gall*. *Gaul* was a territory in western Europe, which was dissolved (brought to an end) militarily by Julius Caesar in the first century BC and eventually became a Roman province. *Gall* is something bitter or distasteful; bitter feeling. The "manufactures of Kentucky" refers to whiskey produced in Kentucky.

drays: low, strong carts without fixed sides, for carrying heavy loads.

Drive: referring to Riverside Drive in New York City, which runs parallel with the Hudson River.

Dutch, in: in trouble or disfavor (with someone).

epistemology: a branch of philosophy that investigates the origin, nature, methods and limits of human knowledge.

faring forth: traveling away from a particular place.

garnishee: to take the money or property of a debtor by legal authority.

G-men: government men; agents of the Federal Bureau of Investigation.

goonies: stupid or foolish people.

hawser: a thick rope or cable for mooring or towing a ship.

jackanapes: somebody who behaves like an ape or monkey.

Ketch, Jack: executioner; an English executioner in the 1600s, notorious for his barbarous inefficiency because he employed either very awkward or sadistic techniques and his victims were known to have suffered at their deaths.

key-jumpy: speaking in a tone of voice characterized by nervous or jittery variations in pitch.

Lady Luck: luck or good fortune represented as a woman.

Lake Tanganyika: a lake in central Africa. It is the longest freshwater lake in the world.

legman: a reporter who gathers information by visiting news sources, or by being present at news events.

loon: a crazy person.

manufactures of Kentucky: whiskey made in Kentucky.

mean: unimposing or shabby.

mill: a typewriter.

morning star: a weapon consisting of a heavy ball, set with spikes and either attached to a staff or suspended from one by a chain.

Mountains of the Moon: a mountain range in central Africa, so called by the natives because of their snowcapped whiteness.

m'sieu: (French) Mr.

non-com: non-commissioned officer; an enlisted person of any of various grades in the armed forces, as from corporal to sergeant major.

obit-ed: a coined word meaning to write an obituary (a notice of a person's death, often with a short biography, in a newspaper).

punch-drunk: befuddled; dazed.

Reds: Communists; also political radicals or revolutionaries.

Scheherazade: the female narrator of *The Arabian Nights,* who during one thousand and one adventurous nights saved her life by entertaining her husband, the king, with stories.

Sea of Dreams: a large dark plain on the far side of the moon that was mistaken by early astronomers for a sea.

semaphores: any of various devices for signaling by changing the position of a light, flag, etc.

senicide: the killing of old men.

septuagenarian: a person who is seventy years of age.

snipes: cigarette butts.

Spinoza: Baruch Spinoza (1632–1677); Dutch philosopher. He claimed to deduce the entire system of thought from a restricted set of definitions and self-evident axioms.

spittoon: a container for spitting into.

stick: a very short article; from an early printing term "composing stick," a hand-held adjustable metal tray in which one set type (a raised letter or other character cast in metal) into words and phrases for printing. One stick only held about ten or twelve lines of type, and a full-page article would be composed using many sticks of type.

stiffen your resolution: to strengthen or make firm one's determination to do something or to carry out a purpose.

swallowtail: a man's fitted coat, cut away over the hips and descending in a pair of tapering skirts behind.

topee: a lightweight hat worn in tropical countries for protection from the sun.

wing collar: a shirt collar, used especially in men's formal clothing, in which the front edges are folded down in such a way as to resemble a pair of wings.

L. Ron Hubbard
in the Golden Age
of Pulp Fiction

*In writing an adventure story
a writer has to know that he is adventuring
for a lot of people who cannot.
The writer has to take them here and there
about the globe and show them
excitement and love and realism.
As long as that writer is living the part of an
adventurer when he is hammering
the keys, he is succeeding with his story.*

*Adventuring is a state of mind.
If you adventure through life, you have a
good chance to be a success on paper.*

*Adventure doesn't mean globe-trotting,
exactly, and it doesn't mean great deeds.
Adventuring is like art.
You have to live it to make it real.*

—*L. RON HUBBARD*

L. Ron Hubbard
and American
Pulp Fiction

B ORN March 13, 1911, L. Ron Hubbard lived a life at least as expansive as the stories with which he enthralled a hundred million readers through a fifty-year career.

Originally hailing from Tilden, Nebraska, he spent his formative years in a classically rugged Montana, replete with the cowpunchers, lawmen and desperadoes who would later people his Wild West adventures. And lest anyone imagine those adventures were drawn from vicarious experience, he was not only breaking broncs at a tender age, he was also among the few whites ever admitted into Blackfoot society as a bona fide blood brother. While if only to round out an otherwise rough and tumble youth, his mother was that rarity of her time—a thoroughly educated woman—who introduced her son to the classics of Occidental literature even before his seventh birthday.

But as any dedicated L. Ron Hubbard reader will attest, his world extended far beyond Montana. In point of fact, and as the son of a United States naval officer, by the age of eighteen he had traveled over a quarter of a million miles. Included therein were three Pacific crossings to a then still mysterious Asia, where he ran with the likes of Her British Majesty's agent-in-place

L. Ron Hubbard, left, at Congressional Airport, Washington, DC, 1931, with members of George Washington University flying club.

for North China, and the last in the line of Royal Magicians from the court of Kublai Khan. For the record, L. Ron Hubbard was also among the first Westerners to gain admittance to forbidden Tibetan monasteries below Manchuria, and his photographs of China's Great Wall long graced American geography texts.

Upon his return to the United States and a hasty completion of his interrupted high school education, the young Ron Hubbard entered George Washington University. There, as fans of his aerial adventures may have heard, he earned his wings as a pioneering barnstormer at the dawn of American aviation. He also earned a place in free-flight record books for the longest sustained flight above Chicago. Moreover, as a roving reporter for *Sportsman Pilot* (featuring his first professionally penned articles), he further helped inspire a generation of pilots who would take America to world airpower.

Immediately beyond his sophomore year, Ron embarked on the first of his famed ethnological expeditions, initially to then untrammeled Caribbean shores (descriptions of which would later fill a whole series of West Indies mystery-thrillers). That the Puerto Rican interior would also figure into the future of Ron Hubbard stories was likewise no accident. For in addition to cultural studies of the island, a 1932–33

124

LRH expedition is rightly remembered as conducting the first complete mineralogical survey of a Puerto Rico under United States jurisdiction.

There was many another adventure along this vein: As a lifetime member of the famed Explorers Club, L. Ron Hubbard charted North Pacific waters with the first shipboard radio direction finder, and so pioneered a long-range navigation system universally employed until the late twentieth century. While not to put too fine an edge on it, he also held a rare Master Mariner's license to pilot any vessel, of any tonnage in any ocean.

Yet lest we stray too far afield, there is an LRH note at this juncture in his saga, and it reads in part:

"I started out writing for the pulps, writing the best I knew, writing for every mag on the stands, slanting as well as I could."

To which one might add: His earliest submissions date from the summer of 1934, and included tales drawn from true-to-life Asian adventures, with characters roughly modeled on British/American intelligence operatives he had known in Shanghai. His early Westerns were similarly peppered with details drawn from personal experience. Although therein lay a first hard lesson from the often cruel world of the pulps. His first Westerns were soundly rejected as lacking the authenticity of a Max Brand yarn

Capt. L. Ron Hubbard in Ketchikan, Alaska, 1940, on his Alaskan Radio Experimental Expedition, the first of three voyages conducted under the Explorers Club flag.

(a particularly frustrating comment given L. Ron Hubbard's Westerns came straight from his Montana homeland, while Max Brand was a mediocre New York poet named Frederick Schiller Faust, who turned out implausible six-shooter tales from the terrace of an Italian villa).

Nevertheless, and needless to say, L. Ron Hubbard persevered and soon earned a reputation as among the most publishable names in pulp fiction, with a ninety percent placement rate of first-draft manuscripts. He was also among the most prolific, averaging between seventy and a hundred thousand words a month. Hence the rumors that L. Ron Hubbard had redesigned a typewriter for faster keyboard action and pounded out manuscripts on a continuous roll of butcher paper to save the precious seconds it took to insert a single sheet of paper into manual typewriters of the day.

That all L. Ron Hubbard stories did not run beneath said byline is yet another aspect of pulp fiction lore. That is, as publishers periodically rejected manuscripts from top-drawer authors if only to avoid paying top dollar, L. Ron Hubbard and company just as frequently replied with submissions under various pseudonyms. In Ron's case, the

A MAN OF MANY NAMES

Between 1934 and 1950, L. Ron Hubbard authored more than fifteen million words of fiction in more than two hundred classic publications. To supply his fans and editors with stories across an array of genres and pulp titles, he adopted fifteen pseudonyms in addition to his already renowned L. Ron Hubbard byline.

Winchester Remington Colt
Lt. Jonathan Daly
Capt. Charles Gordon
Capt. L. Ron Hubbard
Bernard Hubbel
Michael Keith
Rene Lafayette
Legionnaire 148
Legionnaire 14830
Ken Martin
Scott Morgan
Lt. Scott Morgan
Kurt von Rachen
Barry Randolph
Capt. Humbert Reynolds

list included: Rene Lafayette, Captain Charles Gordon, Lt. Scott Morgan and the notorious Kurt von Rachen—supposedly on the lam for a murder rap, while hammering out two-fisted prose in Argentina. The point: While L. Ron Hubbard as Ken Martin spun stories of Southeast Asian intrigue, LRH as Barry Randolph authored tales of

L. Ron Hubbard, circa 1930, at the outset of a literary career that would finally span half a century.

romance on the Western range—which, stretching between a dozen genres is how he came to stand among the two hundred elite authors providing close to a million tales through the glory days of American Pulp Fiction.

In evidence of exactly that, by 1936 L. Ron Hubbard was literally leading pulp fiction's elite as president of New York's American Fiction Guild. Members included a veritable pulp hall of fame: Lester "Doc Savage" Dent, Walter "The Shadow" Gibson, and the legendary Dashiell Hammett—to cite but a few.

Also in evidence of just where L. Ron Hubbard stood within his first two years on the American pulp circuit: By the spring of 1937, he was ensconced in Hollywood, adopting a Caribbean thriller for Columbia Pictures, remembered today as *The Secret of Treasure Island*. Comprising fifteen thirty-minute episodes, the L. Ron Hubbard screenplay led to the most profitable matinée serial in Hollywood history. In accord with Hollywood culture, he was thereafter continually called upon

The 1937 Secret of Treasure Island, *a fifteen-episode serial adapted for the screen by L. Ron Hubbard from his novel,* Murder at Pirate Castle.

to rewrite/doctor scripts—most famously for long-time friend and fellow adventurer Clark Gable.

In the interim—and herein lies another distinctive chapter of the L. Ron Hubbard story—he continually worked to open Pulp Kingdom gates to up-and-coming authors. Or, for that matter, anyone who wished to write. It was a fairly unconventional stance, as markets were already thin and competition razor sharp. But the fact remains, it was an L. Ron Hubbard hallmark that he vehemently lobbied on behalf of young authors—regularly supplying instructional articles to trade journals, guest-lecturing to short story classes at George Washington University and Harvard, and even founding his own creative writing competition. It was established in 1940, dubbed the Golden Pen, and guaranteed winners both New York representation and publication in *Argosy*.

But it was John W. Campbell Jr.'s *Astounding Science Fiction* that finally proved the most memorable LRH vehicle. While every fan of L. Ron Hubbard's galactic epics undoubtedly knows the story, it nonetheless bears repeating: By late 1938, the pulp publishing magnate of Street & Smith was determined to revamp *Astounding Science Fiction* for broader readership. In particular, senior editorial director F. Orlin Tremaine called for stories with a stronger *human element*. When acting editor John W. Campbell balked, preferring his spaceship-driven tales, Tremaine enlisted Hubbard. Hubbard, in turn, replied with the genre's first truly *character-driven* works, wherein heroes are pitted not against bug-eyed monsters but the mystery and majesty of deep space itself—and thus was launched the Golden Age of Science Fiction.

The names alone are enough to quicken the pulse of any science fiction aficionado, including LRH friend and protégé, Robert Heinlein, Isaac Asimov, A. E. van Vogt and Ray Bradbury. Moreover, when coupled with LRH stories of fantasy, we further come to what's rightly been described as the foundation of every modern tale of horror: L. Ron Hubbard's immortal *Fear.* It was rightly proclaimed by Stephen King as one of the very few works to genuinely warrant that overworked term "classic"—as in: *"This is a classic tale of creeping, surreal menace and horror. . . . This is one of the really, really good ones."*

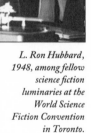

L. Ron Hubbard, 1948, among fellow science fiction luminaries at the World Science Fiction Convention in Toronto.

To accommodate the greater body of L. Ron Hubbard fantasies, Street & Smith inaugurated *Unknown*—a classic pulp if there ever was one, and wherein readers were soon thrilling to the likes of *Typewriter in the Sky* and *Slaves of Sleep* of which Frederik Pohl would declare: *"There are bits and pieces from Ron's work that became part of the language in ways that very few other writers managed."*

And, indeed, at J. W. Campbell Jr.'s insistence, Ron was regularly drawing on themes from the Arabian Nights and

129

so introducing readers to a world of genies, jinn, Aladdin and Sinbad—all of which, of course, continue to float through cultural mythology to this day.

At least as influential in terms of post-apocalypse stories was L. Ron Hubbard's 1940 *Final Blackout*. Generally acclaimed as the finest anti-war novel of the decade and among the ten best works of the genre ever authored—here, too, was a tale that would live on in ways few other writers imagined.

Portland, Oregon, 1943; L. Ron Hubbard, captain of the US Navy subchaser PC 815.

Hence, the later Robert Heinlein verdict: "Final Blackout *is as perfect a piece of science fiction as has ever been written.*"

Like many another who both lived and wrote American pulp adventure, the war proved a tragic end to Ron's sojourn in the pulps. He served with distinction in four theaters and was highly decorated for commanding corvettes in the North Pacific. He was also grievously wounded in combat, lost many a close friend and colleague and thus resolved to say farewell to pulp fiction and devote himself to what it had supported these many years—namely, his serious research.

But in no way was the LRH literary saga at an end, for as he wrote some thirty years later, in 1980:

"Recently there came a period when I had little to do. This was novel in a life so crammed with busy years, and I decided to amuse myself by writing a novel that was pure *science fiction."*

That work was *Battlefield Earth: A Saga of the Year 3000*. It was an immediate *New York Times* bestseller and, in fact, the first international science fiction blockbuster in decades. It was not, however, L. Ron Hubbard's magnum opus, as that distinction is generally reserved for his next and final work: The 1.2 million word *Mission Earth*.

> **Final Blackout**
> *is as perfect a piece of science fiction as has ever been written.*
>
> —Robert Heinlein

How he managed those 1.2 million words in just over twelve months is yet another piece of the L. Ron Hubbard legend. But the fact remains, he did indeed author a ten-volume *dekalogy* that lives in publishing history for the fact that each and every volume of the series was also a *New York Times* bestseller.

Moreover, as subsequent generations discovered L. Ron Hubbard through republished works and novelizations of his screenplays, the mere fact of his name on a cover signaled an international bestseller. . . . Until, to date, sales of his works exceed hundreds of millions, and he otherwise remains among the most enduring and widely read authors in literary history. Although as a final word on the tales of L. Ron Hubbard, perhaps it's enough to simply reiterate what editors told readers in the glory days of American Pulp Fiction:

He writes the way he does, brothers, because he's been there, seen it and done it!

THE STORIES FROM THE GOLDEN AGE

Your ticket to adventure starts here with the Stories from
the Golden Age collection by master storyteller L. Ron Hubbard.
These gripping tales are set in a kaleidoscope of exotic locales and brim
with fascinating characters, including some of the
most vile villains, dangerous dames and brazen heroes
you'll ever get to meet.

The entire collection of over one hundred and fifty stories is being
released in a series of eighty books and audiobooks.
For an up-to-date listing of available titles,
go to www.goldenagestories.com.

AIR ADVENTURE

Arctic Wings	*Man-Killers of the Air*
The Battling Pilot	*On Blazing Wings*
Boomerang Bomber	*Red Death Over China*
The Crate Killer	*Sabotage in the Sky*
The Dive Bomber	*Sky Birds Dare!*
Forbidden Gold	*The Sky-Crasher*
Hurtling Wings	*Trouble on His Wings*
The Lieutenant Takes the Sky	*Wings Over Ethiopia*

FAR-FLUNG ADVENTURE

SEA ADVENTURE

TALES FROM THE ORIENT

MYSTERY

135

FANTASY

SCIENCE FICTION

WESTERN